SCORING CHANCE

TEAGAN HUNTER

Editing by Editing by C. Marie

Proofreading by Judy's Proofreading & Julia Griffis

Cover Design by Emily Wittig Designs

To the Marine.
You're the only one I want to score with.
Well, most of the time.
I mean, have you seen some of the hockey players?

CHAPTER 1

"You're a *what*?!"

I wince at the level-ten volume at which he screams the words. I yank my hat down lower and glance around to ensure we haven't drawn any unwanted attention. Luckily, we're so far out of the way from others that I don't think anyone heard him. This is not the kind of information I want to spread around.

"You heard me," I tell Greer, my teammate and the starting goalie for the Carolina Comets.

"I'm not entirely sure I did, so let's start from the beginning." He points to himself. "I said I was going to town on some chick last night, and somehow, she reached around and stuck her finger in my ass." He stretches his finger my way. "Then I asked if that's ever happened to you, and you said—"

"No, I'm a virgin."

His mouth drops open at the confirmation, and the donut he's holding slips from between his fingers, splatting icing side first onto the table—a shame, especially since I know the Chocolate Nutty Butter is the best donut ever created. He's staring at me like I'm crazy, like there has to be some miscommunication going on.

There isn't.

I'm a twenty-four-year-old professional hockey player…and a virgin.

I'm a fucking anomaly.

"I… What… I can't even comprehend this right now. How did I not know this?"

I shrug. "It's not exactly something I advertise."

"How?"

"Huh?"

"How?" Greer repeats.

I didn't think I'd have to explain this to him, but… "Well, it's simple—I've never stuck my dick in a woman before. I—"

"No, you idiot. That part I understand just fine. What I mean is *how*? How in the fuck have you not had sex yet? You're what, twenty-three?"

"Twenty-four." I don't bother to remind him he was at my birthday dinner just last month.

"Fuck, man." He shakes his head. "How?"

I don't want to get into my reasoning because I know it sounds stupid. I've already told him enough, so I settle for, "I don't know, man. Just never happened." Then I pray he lets it go.

Like, I legit close my eyes and clasp my hands

together. My grandmother would be so proud if she could see me right now. She was always wanting me to become more religious. I think praying my friend and teammate doesn't continue to question my lack of dicking down a woman counts, right?

I have no idea how long passes before he finally says, "Okay, how do we fix this?"

Slowly, I peel one eye open, then the other. "Fix what?"

"Your..." He waves his hand toward me. "*Issue.*"

I'm not too keen on the way he says *issue*. I'm a virgin —big damn deal. There's nothing wrong with being one. I'm not embarrassed by it at all. I'm just...frustrated— and not just sexually. I'm frustrated because I've gotten to this point in my life and let so many things pass me by.

Prom? Never went.

Skipping school? As if I'd ever let that shit go on my record.

Girlfriends? I wasn't about to let my GPA suffer because of someone I was dating.

I lived and breathed hockey. My days consisted of four AM practices before school and running drills afterward until well into the night. My weekends were games and tournaments. When it wasn't hockey season, I was practicing for hockey season.

The game always came first because I had dreams, big ones. And they came true.

I'm lucky, and I know that. I get to play the best game

in the world in the best league. But now that I'm here, I can't help but think maybe I gave up just a little bit too much for these dreams.

"It's not a big deal," I mumble, even though it feels like one, especially when he's staring at me like I'm King Ghidorah or some other three-headed monster.

"If you don't care about it, why'd you tell me? I wouldn't have known otherwise." He lifts a challenging brow, picking up the remnants of his dropped donut and shoveling it into his mouth.

Fuck. He's got me there.

I clasp my hand around the back of my neck, trying to squeeze out the tension that's slowly building.

Why the fuck *did* I tell Greer? I could have easily lied to him. Hell, I probably should have. He's by far the biggest asshole on the team. I mean, not that he's *really* an asshole. He's just honest, and some people don't like that. His honesty doesn't bother me, though. For someone who has been used most of their life, it's refreshing to have someone be honest.

"Is it bothering you?" he guesses when I don't answer immediately. "Messing with your game at all?"

"Most of the time, no."

"But it *does* bother you?"

I sigh. "Of course it does. I turned twenty-four a month ago, and I'm ninety-nine percent positive I may be the oldest virgin in the entire history of the NHL. It's hard not to think about it sometimes. I can score on the ice all damn day, but I can't score off it? It's sad."

"It's not sad. It's life, and sometimes life is shit." He says it like he's speaking from experience, and maybe he is. We only just recently started hanging out, and I don't know much about Greer's life, but he's not exactly easy to read. I always figure if he wants me to know something about him, he'll tell me, so I don't pry. "We can fix this. We just need to teach you to talk to women."

"I know how to talk to women, fucker. I never said that was my problem. And besides, I don't need your help."

That damn brow of his rises again like he doesn't believe me. Shit, if I were sitting across from me right now discussing losing my virginity at twenty-four, I wouldn't believe me either.

"You're telling me you've never been with a woman, and I—"

"Just because I've never had sex doesn't mean I've never been with a woman. I've been with plenty."

All right, fine, so *plenty* is a significant stretch. I've fooled around some but not much else.

"When's the last time you were with one, then?" he challenges.

"Last night."

"Who?"

"Your mom."

He drops his head, shaking it. "I walked right into that, huh?" He scrubs his hand over his face. "This is going to be a lot more work than I thought."

"Again, I don't need your help."

"Says the virgin."

It's not that I'm entirely hopeless with women. I can flirt. I can charm. I've had plenty of dates over the last few years.

Sure, nothing has stuck, but that doesn't mean I need dating help. I think it just means I need to find the right person to date, and I certainly don't need Greer's help with that.

"What about her?" Greer lifts his chin toward someone.

I follow his line of sight to the front of the donut truck we're sitting outside of. Inside is the truck's owner, the woman who happens to make the best damn donuts I've ever had.

She also happens to hate me.

"Her name is Scout," I tell him, turning back around.

"You know her, then?"

I shrug. "Sort of. She's, uh, not a big fan of mine."

"What'd you do?"

"Why do you assume it was something I did?"

"Because I once watched you hit on a mom *and* her daughter. You're not exactly smooth with the ladies."

Fuck. I did do that.

I drag my hand back to my neck, squeezing it again because more tension is building. I'll have to see about stopping by the team's masseuse if this shit keeps up. I need to be loose on the ice, not all keyed up like this.

I groan. "I sort of…introduced myself to her."

His brows slam together. "Is that a bad thing?"

"Since I come here pretty much weekly and should have known who she was, yes."

Even Greer winces at that, and he should. It was embarrassing as hell.

In all fairness, I'm used to seeing her from the tits up with her brown hair tossed into a bun and an apron on. I didn't expect to see her at my former teammate's party wearing a dress that hugged all her curves with curled hair and the sexiest fucking smoky eyes I've ever seen.

"Yeah, okay. Maybe not her." His eyes slide back toward the truck. "Or..." He draws the word out. "Maybe yes her, because she's definitely looking this way right now."

I'm almost sure he's screwing with me, so I glance over my shoulder to check. Before I can get a good look, Greer smacks me in the back of the head.

"Don't look, you idiot. It'll make it obvious that we're talking about her."

"Ouch." I rub the spot he hit. "Fine, I won't look."

"I won't lie, you are missing out."

I go to sneak a glance, and he hits me again.

"Stop hitting me, asshole."

"Well, stop looking. Breaking your neck to get a glimpse makes you look more desperate than you already are."

"Fuck you. I'm not desperate."

"You wouldn't be coming to me for help if that wasn't the case."

"But I'm *not* coming to you for help. You've just inserted yourself into this."

"Because this can't go on any longer. You're a fucking pro hockey player and a damn good one at that—you should be swimming in pussy."

"Like you are with your ass-play girlfriend?"

"First of all, she's not my girlfriend." He wrinkles his nose like the thought is disgusting to him. "I don't do girlfriends. I'm not really the relationship type. Tried it, wasn't for me."

"I've never had a girlfriend."

There I go confessing more shit to him like he's my fucking therapist or something.

"Seriously? You're a virgin *and* you've never even had a girlfriend before?"

I shake my head, hoping like hell he doesn't see the heat that's definitely filling my cheeks right now because this shit is embarrassing to talk about. "No. I, uh, spent a lot of time playing hockey."

What I don't tell him is I tried to date in high school, but as soon as my dad found out, he nixed that completely. Girls were distractions, and I wasn't allowed to be distracted. I had to keep my eye on the prize: the NHL.

I got drafted right after high school and wasn't in college long enough to get wild. By then, dating and girls and everything else felt like too much pressure, and with having to prove to the Comets that I was call-up worthy, I was already under enough. I've certainly made up for it over the last few years, but it's not like I'm out with a different woman every night the way he seems to be.

"So did I, but I still made time for pussy. Tell me you've at least had your dick sucked."

"Why? You offering if not?" He glowers at me, and I laugh. "Yeah, I've had my dick sucked."

"Well, at least you've experienced that. Was it any good?"

I mean, I came, but would I say good... Eh.

Apparently, I don't have to tell him that; my face must say it all.

He chucks his third donut, which is only half eaten, back into the box. "You're depressing me and ruining my donuts." He glances over my shoulder. "But not as much as she's depressing me."

I risk the smack to my head and look this time. The heated stare Scout is sending my way makes me scared she's about to pull a knife from behind her back and chase me out of the parking lot with it.

I shift around on the bench because, sadly, a tiny part of me finds that particular scenario really hot.

Shit. Maybe I am more desperate to get laid than I thought.

Scout is in her usual attire: an apron over a pair of overalls with her hair piled high on top of her head in the same messy look. Her usually pouty lips are rolled together, and she's standing with her arms crossed over her ample chest. She looks just as annoyed as she was at the party.

And even more so when she realizes *I'm* now staring at *her*.

I lift my hand in a small wave, and the frown she's sporting deepens. It takes half a second for her to turn her back on me, busying herself with something in the truck. It's clear to anyone else watching that she's not actually working on anything and is just ignoring me.

Guess I deserve the cold shoulder.

"Wow." Greer whistles. "You weren't kidding. She does hate you. It looks like you might be screwed when it comes to her, and not in the way you're hoping to be. It's too bad, too. She's hot, maybe a little nerdy for me, but the nerdy girls are always up for some kinky shit." He bounces his brows up and down, grinning. "I bet she'd forgive you if you played the famous hockey player card."

His words grate on every damn nerve I have because I swear he sounds just like my father right now.

I've been *the hockey player* my entire life. It's all my parents ever cared about since they realized I wasn't so bad at the game. Having me go pro became their life, so it became *my* life. So much so that I gave up everything—and I do mean everything—for it, and none of it was for the right reasons.

I'm not telling Greer any of that shit, though. I've already said entirely too much.

"I'm more than a hockey player." The words come out much harsher than I intended.

He doesn't miss it either, his eyes widening at my sudden outburst.

He lifts his hands in surrender. "Didn't say you weren't. I'm just saying it's not a bad card to use. Works like a fucking charm for me." He licks remnants of his donut—Fruit & Pebbles this time—off his fingers. "Shit, maybe I should hit her up because damn these donuts are good."

My stomach sours at the thought of Greer and Scout together. I don't have any business having any sort of opinion about it, but still, I don't like it for some reason. Maybe because Scout's always seemed nice, and Greer is a bit of a tool on a good day. Plus, it's clear all he wants women for is one thing, and Scout doesn't deserve that.

"You shouldn't want people just for what they're good at."

He pauses just before he takes a bite of his fourth donut, then quirks a brow. "I'm sensing there's some unresolved shit going on with you given the comments you've made, but I'm not going to go into it because I'm a respectful asshole."

"You've got the asshole part right," I say, and he just laughs, completely unfazed.

"That I am." He grabs a napkin and wipes the remaining mess off his hands. "All right, if we're done bonding for the day, I'm heading out. I need to stop by the practice barn and check out my new helmet." He rises, towering over the table with a stern look. "We're not done talking about this, though—the virgin thing, I mean. We need to get that fixed."

"We?"

"Yup. Can't have you out on the ice in these conditions. It's clearly eating you up. We don't need you distracted. We got a Cup to win, baby."

He's not wrong about that.

"And that," he says, nodding toward the truck. "Fix that."

"Scout?"

"Yes. I'd like to enjoy my breakfast peacefully and not feel like I'm about two seconds away from being chased off with a broom. You need to apologize to her."

"I've tried," I explain. "Several times. She hides or puts up her *Be Right Back* sign and then never returns. Hell, she even shoved a kid to the register once."

"Try again. Nobody wants to eat donuts in these conditions."

"Fine. I'll talk to her." I rise to my feet. "But I just have one question before you go."

"What's that?"

"Did you like it?"

"Huh?"

I lift one finger in the air, wiggling it around with a grin. "Did you like it?"

His cheeks pinken, and he looks about two seconds away from leaping over the table and swinging at me, but he can't. We're in public, and Coach would have our asses if we got in trouble for fighting.

So instead, he flips me off, which makes me laugh even harder.

I swear I hear him call me a dick as he heads for the makeshift parking lot.

With a sigh, I pick up our trash and head for the garbage cans up front, readying myself for my second embarrassment of the day: apologizing to Scout.

She can't hide from me forever, right?

CHAPTER 2

Some things in life genuinely suck.

Having a piece of food stuck in your teeth and nobody telling you. A bird crapping on your car as soon as you wash it for the first time in months. Not being recognized by your crush.

That last one?

It happened to me. Just two weeks ago, actually.

Now that same guy is walking toward my food truck, and what the hell am I doing?

Hiding.

As in I am physically ducked down and hiding because he caught me staring at him not once but twice today. Now he's coming up here presumably to talk, something I want no part of.

"What the hell are you doing?" Stevie asks. She's my older sister, and today she's also my savior for bailing me out and helping in the truck this morning when my other baker flaked on me for the second time this month. I'm really starting to think I need different help.

Stevie stares down at me with her brows pulled tight together, her hazel eyes narrowed in confusion as she waits for me to answer.

What am I supposed to tell her? That I'm hiding from the ridiculously hot hockey player who's walking this way? Not going to happen. I'll sound insane for so many reasons.

"I'm… Inventory," I tell her.

"*You're* inventory?"

"Yes. Well, I'm *doing* inventory. We need more nutmeg."

She crosses her arms over her chest, a smirk forming on her lips, clearly amused by me making a complete and utter fool of myself. "Nutmeg?"

"The nuttiest of meg," I answer.

She laughs. "Get up, you weirdo. A customer is coming. Are you… Oh!" Realization dawns on Stevie's face, and she drops down next to me. "Are you hiding from *him*?"

"Yes!" I whisper, though it comes out as more of a hiss.

"Why?" Stevie questions. "Wait—is that *the guy*?"

I nod reluctantly.

Stevie knows all about *The Guy*.

The Guy who, when I first saw him, I swore was the most beautiful man I'd ever seen.

The Guy who, when I first talked to him, made me more tongue-tied than I've ever been before, and I've met three of the Backstreet Boys *and* Keanu Reeves, thank you very much.

The Guy who makes my heart flutter.

And The Guy who, despite coming to my donut truck almost weekly for the last year, doesn't seem to have a single damn clue who I am.

"Is it safe to assume your crush on him is still going strong if you're hiding?"

"No. I'm hiding because he's a jerk," I counter. "And I do *not* have a crush on him."

It's a lie, and we both know it.

Can I be blamed, though? He's Grady Miller, star right winger for the Carolina Comets. Not only is he incredible and charismatic on the ice, he's also the same way off it. I can't count the number of times he's been bombarded by rabid fans here at my truck, and he just smiles, signs all the things, and takes countless photos with them. I've also seen him order a box of donuts and share it with Eddie, the man who sits on the corner just up the street, never once slinging an ounce of judgment his way.

And just because that couldn't possibly be enough, he has to go and be the hottest man I've ever seen. If he weren't a hockey player, I have no doubt he could be a model with his midnight black hair that's always messy like he just rolled out of bed and a jawline so damn sharp the TSA should consider it a weapon. And his eyes... It's as if someone poured a tumbler of top-shelf whiskey right into them.

I shouldn't be crushing on him. He's so far out of my league that we're not even playing the same sport.

He's an NHL player. I'm a donut maker. There's no way we would ever make any sense together.

My little crush on him? It's a fantasy, just like what I read about in novels. I never had any intention of doing anything about it, and now I'm confident I never will after the incident two weeks ago where he introduced himself to me like he doesn't stop by my donut truck regularly.

"I still can't believe he didn't recognize you," Stevie says.

I can. I can believe it because it's what has happened to me all my life.

I'm invisible. People don't *see* me. They never really have.

I'm the girl in the background of every movie who is just out of the camera's focus, watching while the popular girl gets the popular guy. I'm not saying that to hate on myself, and I'm not saying it because I don't think I'm attractive enough or worth getting—because I am on both counts. I'm saying it because it's true. I play it safe and don't step out of my comfort zone. I'm good with being safe and remaining the background or secondary character. I'm content with my life.

But sometimes…just sometimes…I wish I weren't.

I wish I were more outgoing. Wish I weren't so damn awkward. Wish I had the guts to do something brave, like writing the romance novel like I promised I would and finally publishing it.

But I'm none of those things, because the idea of becoming or doing them makes me want to vomit.

I'm just Scout: donut maker, nerd, and wannabe writer.

And I'm okay with that.

"You can't hide from him forever, you know," Stevie tells me.

"Yes, I can."

She chuckles lightly, brushing brown hair that almost exactly matches mine behind her ear. "You made my nine-year-old daughter work the register for thirty minutes when he was here the other day. I'm pretty sure there are child labor laws against that or something."

"It's not my fault he wouldn't go away."

"Scout..."

"Steve," I say, knowing she hates it when I call her that, but I hate that she's calling me out on my childish behavior. I guess stooping to juvenile insults isn't helping my case, but still.

"You have to talk to him sometime."

She really has no clue how humiliating it was, though. I'd never felt like such an outsider before. It took everything I had not to drop off the donuts and leave because it was so damn clear to me that even though I considered some of those people my friends, I didn't belong there.

I'm not their friend. I'm their donut maker, and they are customers. That's it.

"You need to talk to him, and I'm not bailing you out this time." She pushes up to her feet, then begins untying the apron that's slung around her waist.

"What?! Where are you going?"

"I told you…" she says, sliding the apron onto the hook near the exit. "Macie has a dentist appointment."

"No! Cancel it! Reschedule! I don't care—just don't leave me."

She pulls her crossbody purse over her head, then looks at me like she can't believe I just said that. Hell, *I* can't believe I just said it. It's stupid. I'm being stupid.

"Just talk to him," she says again, then she steps out of the back of the truck like the traitor she is.

Here I was thinking she was here to do good, but this? It's evil. *She's* evil.

"Stevie!" I whisper-shout at her back despite knowing damn well she's not going to turn around and help me. Stevie loves tough love. I'm surprised she's let me get away with this little game of mine as long as she has.

I watch her walk away from my crouched position and don't miss her sending a wave to someone standing at the front of the truck.

Does that mean…

"Are you hiding from me?"

Oh crap.

"Because you know…" he continues, tapping the

countertop a few times, "I'm tall. I can see over this thing, and I can definitely see you."

Dammit.

"You can't avoid me forever."

Can too.

"Even Stevie said you can't."

With a heavy sigh, I rise, and yep, he's there all right, in all his perfect hockey-player hotness. He's grinning at me, and it's annoying because somehow even his teeth are perfect.

"Ah, there she is," he says.

His voice is laced with sugary sweetness, but I'm not buying it. I've been fooled by men with pretty faces before.

"What do you want." It doesn't come out as a question because all the niceties I had are gone when it comes to Miller.

He grimaces, his bravado slipping away before my eyes. He rocks back on his heels as one hand goes to his pocket and the other comes up to his neck. He cups it, squeezing like he's trying to relieve tension. It almost makes me feel bad.

Almost.

"I, uh…" He clears his throat. "Well, I'd like to apologize."

I lift a brow. "For?"

"Smith's party."

I cross my arms over my chest. "What about Smith's party?"

He swallows thickly. "Fornotrecognizingyou."

It comes out rushed as one word, like he's embarrassed. Which I'm glad for because, given the number of times he has been to my truck, he *should* be embarrassed.

He blows out a breath like he's relieved to get the words off his chest. I'm glad one of us is relieved by this, but it's not me. I'm still humiliated by what happened.

"It was very dickish of me."

"Dickish is a good way to put it. Personally, I would have said you were being an asshole, but dickish is fine too."

A smirk plays at the corner of his lips, and I'm annoyed by how cute I think it is, especially when I'm supposed to be mad at him. "I've never seen you outside of here," he says by way of explanation. "It was... Well, you didn't look like *you*."

"I'm not sure if I'm supposed to be offended by that."

"Not!" he practically yells. "Not. I mean it in a good way."

My brows pull together because... "Are you saying I look bad when I'm here?"

"Yes." He nods, but somewhere along the way, his movements switch from up and down to left and right as his eyes widen to about twice their average size. "No, no, no! That's not what I'm saying. You look great, now and then—just different."

"Different?" My lips twitch, perhaps because I'm

enjoying watching him trip over himself just a little too much right now.

He sighs, scrubbing a hand over his face before looking up at me with tired eyes. "Look, I'm an idiot sometimes, okay? I do and say stupid things. That's the only excuse I really have as to why I didn't recognize you. That and I'm pretty sure my grandmother had glaucoma, and that shit is hereditary. I think...I don't know. I saw a meme one time that said that, so maybe my eyes are going bad. I swear I'll make an appointment with the team doctor ASAP, just to be sure. I..." He takes another heavy breath. "I'm just sorry, all right? I'm so, so sorry."

He stares up at me with those whiskey-colored eyes that are silently begging me to believe him.

The sad part is that it's working. I can see this is eating him up.

He *has* tried to talk to me several times. Maybe he means it, and maybe he meant nothing by it. In all fairness, I did look really different that night.

Perhaps I'm stupid or weak, or maybe that silly crush of mine might not totally be gone, but...

"Okay," I say, letting him off the hook. "I forgive you."

He exhales sharply, pressing his hand against his chest. "Oh, thank fuck. Because I really want you to forgive me. I love coming here, and I'm pretty sure I can't live without your donuts."

"That so, huh?"

"Hell yes. I'm addicted to the——"

"Chocolate Nutty Butter. I know."

He looks surprised. "You do?"

"Yes, because unlike you, I remember people."

His jaw drops for a moment, shock rippling through him. Then he chuckles, but I can hear the hurt in it. I feel just a tiny bit bad, but dammit, he hurt my feelings too.

"I deserved that."

"You really did," I agree.

"Truce? No more hiding from me?"

"I wasn't hiding," I insist. "I was doing inventory."

"Right." He smirks. "Inventory."

"We need nutmeg," I say defiantly, but it's a lie. We have plenty of nutmeg.

Luckily, he doesn't call me out on it.

"I'm glad you finally talked to me. I'm glad we can be friends."

I snort out a laugh. "I never said anything about being friends."

His eyes widen again, and he takes an actual step back like I've just knocked all the wind out of his sails. "Are you saying you don't want to be my friend?"

"That's exactly what I'm saying."

"Why not?"

"Well, for starters, you forgot who I am..."

He groans. "I told you, I'm——"

"An idiot. Yeah, I picked up on that. But secondly, you don't really want to be friends with me."

"Yes, I do."

"No, you really don't. We have no business being friends."

"Why not? You're friends with Lowell, aren't you? Smith too, so why not me?"

Do I know Lowell better than the other guys? Yes, but only because we went to high school together, and Smith is only friendly toward me because my niece has some sort of weird attachment to him. She's obsessed with hockey and idolizes the guy ever since he sponsored her soccer team.

"Because we're two totally different people, Miller."

"Grady," he says. "That's what my friends call me."

"Yeah, that's what you said at Smith's party." He looks sheepish again, a tinge of red popping back up on his cheeks. "But we're not friends, so you're just Miller the hockey player to me."

A dark look crosses his features, and it's almost as if I've hurt his feelings.

Then, almost as quickly as it came, it's gone, and he's grinning again. "You're going to be my friend, Scout."

"I'm really not."

"You will." His smile widens, and it even reaches his eyes this time. "I'm going to come here every day until you agree to be friends with me," he promises.

The thought of having to see Miller every day has my stomach in knots because I'm not sure if my lady bits can stand it. Hell, they're barely able to stand it right now with the way he's grinning up at me. How is it possible he's this attractive?

I scramble for a reason to get him to stay away.

"I don't think your coaches would like you eating donuts every day," I rush out.

"Probably not." He pats his flat stomach. "But I think I can work it off."

I'm sure he's not lying either. I've gone ice-skating a few times, and every single lap ended with me being winded. I can't imagine the skill it takes to handle a stick, chase a puck, and get hit by other large dudes, all while trying not to die from exhaustion.

"What if I kick you out?"

"Then I'll sit across the street."

Dammit. Why does he always have to have an answer for everything?

"What if I never become your friend?"

"That's not really something we'll have to worry about."

Another grin—another zing right between my thighs.

My face starts to heat up, and I swear it just got ten degrees hotter outside.

Goodness gracious. Get it together, Scout.

"Anyone ever tell you you're cocky, *Miller?*"

"Confident, not cocky." He taps the counter a few times. "I'll be back tomorrow, *Scout.*"

"Uh-huh. I'll believe it when I see it."

He shoots me one last grin before turning on his heel and trudging to the parking lot toward the shiny, fancy sports car he's always driving way too fast.

I watch him the entire time. Every stride he takes, every rock he kicks...I see it.

Which is why I don't miss him turning back my way once he reaches his car and shooting me a wave.

And I don't miss the way my heart flutters at the little movement either.

I pray he doesn't come back...because I'm not sure how long I'll last.

CHAPTER 3

"Come on, Miller. Get those fucking legs moving. We need speed, speed, speed!"

I clench my teeth and push my legs harder at Coach's request. I know I can do it. I can get to where he wants me to be, but, fuck, my legs are tired as hell.

It's always grueling getting back into the game after taking time off. Not that I actually take time off, but when it's not hockey season, my time on the ice is significantly reduced, and right now, I'm feeling it everywhere. My thighs, my ass, my lower back—all of it is aching.

But I need to push because we have a lot riding on this season after our first-round exit last year. We need to prove to everyone that we aren't just a one-Cup-and-done team. We need to prove we can do it and are here to stay at the top of this league.

"That's it! Tape to tape, boys," Coach hollers when I smack the puck to Lowell and it lands on his stick effortlessly. We're in sync, which is a good damn start for our first day back at it.

Lowell takes the puck to the net, trying to get Greer to bite on it. He does, and that's when Lowell sends the puck my way, then I shoot it straight to the back of the net.

Lowell skates over to me with his glove out, and I bump mine against his. "Nice fucking play, kid. A perfect read."

It was, especially considering we didn't practice this at all. While I'm damn proud of what we just did, I'm a little worried about Greer biting on the fake-out. Those are the small things that can really blow a game for us.

Greer doesn't look happy about it, but in typical fashion, he doesn't let it show beyond the glower on his face. Even under pressure and when he fucks up, he takes it in stride and keeps pushing. That's what keeps my hope up that just maybe we'll be okay.

"From the top!" Coach yells, and we all take our positions again.

We run the play once more. This time, Greer's ready for it, and he beats us glove side.

The next line hits the ice, and we take our places on the bench.

"Fuck, my legs are killing me," Rhodes, our biggest and meanest defenseman, comments as he gulps in breath after breath.

"Dude, you're telling me. This shit is exhausting.

Remind me again why we do this?" says Wright, another defenseman and Rhodes' partner.

"Because we love the hurt," Lowell answers. "And money."

They all grin, because our captain's not wrong. That's exactly why we do it.

I still remember the first time I stepped onto the ice. Well, step is a nice way of putting it. I fell, like immediately went down on my ass. It hurt, but the embarrassment that crossed my father's face hurt more. So, I didn't say shit. I just got up and tried again. I went down so many times that day, but I never gave up. Instead, I asked to go back again sometime. My dad liked my determination and took me. This time there were some older kids playing hockey. They invited me over and handed me a stick. Even though I'd never played or even watched a game before, I went all in. I loved every damn minute of it.

It took me a bit to get used to it, but once I was in, I was all the way in. And I wasn't bad at it either.

When we wrapped up the game, one of the other dads said to mine, "I don't say this lightly: that kid has potential—big potential. I'd get him on the right path if I were you."

That's how it all started. Afterward, hockey became everything to me, and the bragging rights and money that came with making it pro became everything to my family.

Even knowing now that all I am is a pawn to them, I

wouldn't trade it, because I really do love the game that much.

"How the hell are you even out here kicking so much ass with a baby at home?" Wright says to Lowell.

"Because my baby momma is a fucking rockstar and is killing it." He grins, looking so damn proud of his girlfriend, Hollis. "And because my daughter is an angel."

Rhodes huffs. "I beg to differ."

"You're only saying that because she spit up on you twice," Lowell says. "If you'd stop scowling at her, maybe she'd like you more."

"I don't scowl at her," the man in question argues... while scowling.

"You do too, but you can't really help it. It's just your default setting," Wright tells him. He shakes his head. "I still have no idea how you and Ryan got together. She's like the polar opposite of you."

Just the mention of Rhodes' wife has his infamous scowl turning into a grin. He's so smitten with her. But it really is just like Wright says—they're opposites in every way. She's the Beauty to his Beast, and it works for them.

"Unlike you and Harper," Lowell says to Wright. "You're basically the same weird horror-obsessed people."

"Hey, she's way more into it than I am. You won't believe her latest request and what she wants me to do with that Michael Myers mask. She—"

Lowell holds his hand up to stop him. "Nope. Don't

want to hear about anything you do with Hollis' sister. That's my daughter's aunt. I'm good."

"Yeah, but you used to *love* hearing about all our weird shit before you got with her sister."

"And now I don't. It's just...weird. You're too much like family."

"Did you just call me your brother?"

Lowell scowls at the idea, and I laugh, which draws some attention my way.

"What about you, Miller? We all got taken down by love. When's it your turn?"

I try not to react or slink back in my seat. I'm still trying to forget that conversation with Greer yesterday about the sad state of my love life.

Wright nods toward Smith, who is staring intently at what's happening on the ice. "Even the old grump found someone."

"Yeah, someone he definitely wasn't supposed to be looking for," Lowell mutters.

"Can you imagine what it's like sitting around that dinner table? With your former coach turned colleague, who also happens to be your girlfriend's uncle?" Rhodes shakes his head. "I can't even imagine that dynamic."

"Like you're one to talk, Beast. Now you have to explain to your future children that you drunk-wed their mother in Vegas."

"Well, technically..." Rhodes starts, but Wright waves him off.

"Technically my ass. At least Harper and I have a normal story to tell our nieces and nephews."

"First of all, there was nothing normal about how you and Harper met," Lowell says. "Secondly, are you and Harper still in the No Kids camp?"

"Yep," he answers proudly. "We're good being the fun aunt and uncle. Which reminds me—we bought baby Freddie this adorable little glove with knife hands."

Lowell huffs. "She's named after Freddie Mercury, not Freddy Krueger, you weirdo."

"Semantics."

Not that I'd admit it out loud or anything because the guys would roast me until the end of time, but I kind of love watching them talk about their women. It's refreshing. My dad never talked about my mom the way these guys talk about their ladies. He'd always roll his eyes or have something shitty to say about her, and then degrade her in some way. She'd take it out on me, of course, but that's a whole other box of shit I'm not ready to deal with right now.

And I wouldn't dare say this either, but I think a big part of why I haven't been able to just lose my virginity to any random woman is because after watching these guys fall in love one by one, I don't want her to be random.

I want what they all have.

"On the ice, fellas!" Smith calls out, interrupting us.

It's still so weird to see him behind the bench, especially when we were just out here playing with him a few months ago. I know he's going to be missed this season. Whoever is coming into his position has some big skates to fill.

We pile back over the boards and take our positions at center ice. We run through a few more drills, working on some plays but mostly just getting a feel for being back on the ice and together again.

It's exhausting, but it's fun. It feels damn good to be out here playing the game I love so much with the guys I've grown to consider family. I don't have any brothers, so this is the closest I'll ever get to having them.

We wrap up practice for the day, then hit the weights for a quick thirty-minute workout. After that, we gather in the meeting room to go over all the not-so-fun stuff we need to get done this season. I really thought hockey was just going to be about playing the game, but there's so much more that goes into it.

"And that brings us to our annual start-of-the-season fundraiser. As usual, all proceeds will go toward Kid Comets. We'd like to beat the total we donated last year by at least ten thousand. The black-tie charity event is in three weeks, and everyone is required to attend. Plus-ones are not mandatory, but it is encouraged since we need those donations. So bring your dates and bring your checkbooks, boys." Coach stacks his papers together and closes the cover of his notebook. "Practice is at eight sharp tomorrow. If you need anything else, you know where to find me."

With that, he heads for the door, leaving us to ourselves for the day.

"You going to bring a date?" Greer asks, popping up beside me. "If you can get one, I mean."

I glare at him. "I can get one."

"That's not what your track record says."

I glance around, making sure nobody is paying any attention to us. "Shut up."

"Why? Afraid they'll learn you're not the ladies' man you claim to be?"

All right, fine. So maybe all the guys on the team think I date around more than I let on. And I guess I do go on a lot of dates with a lot of girls I never call back. When the guys ask about it, I always give them a cocky grin and say I never kiss and tell.

But the truth is, there's never anything to tell because nothing usually happens on those dates.

Greer laughs, clapping me on the shoulder and steering me out of the room. "I'm just screwing with you, man. I'd never say anything about…your *thing*."

For some reason, I believe him. Greer may be an asshole and he may love fucking with me, but I also trust him.

"I think we're going to hit up Slapshots. Guess it's tradition or something. Want to come?"

Going to the hockey-themed bar downtown is a team ritual, but today I have something I have to do first.

"I'll meet you guys there later." For a moment, I contemplate telling Greer where I'm headed, but I don't want to field the million and one questions he's going to have, especially after yesterday.

"Sure, man. No problem. Text me when you're on your way."

I nod, then head in the opposite direction. In the parking garage, I climb into my gray Porsche 911 Turbo S, firing it up and relishing the way she purrs to life under me. I've never been a big car guy, but the moment I saw this beauty, I knew I had to have her. Besides, me spending the money on myself really pissed my dad off, which made me love the car ten times more.

I send the gate guard a wave as I squeal out of the garage and head toward my destination. Less than ten minutes later, I'm pulling into the makeshift parking lot and throwing the car into park.

I grab my trusty Comets baseball cap and tug it down over my head before hopping out of the car. The place is empty for the moment, but I'm sure people are going to start showing up any time now for their midday pick-me-up.

I head straight for the person I came here to see, and the moment she spots me, she lets out a long, exaggerated sigh and lifts her eyes skyward.

I think I'm supposed to be offended by how unhappy she is to see me, but I can't be, not when I know Scout doesn't really hate me. She wants to be my friend, and I want to be hers. Outside of my teammates, I don't really know anyone else here, and it would be nice to talk to someone about something other than hockey sometimes.

Hell, even all the girls I've tried dating are only interested in one thing—the game. For once, I want to talk to someone who doesn't just see me as a hockey player. I want them to just see me, and based on the way she doesn't seem to give a flying fuck about who I am, Scout just might be that person I'm looking for.

I laugh, then send her a wave. "Heya, friend. How's your day?"

She gives me a pointed glare. "Still not friends, Miller."

"Sure we are, and as your friend, I'm here to support your small local business. Can I please get a black coffee with—"

"One packet of sugar and a shake of cinnamon."

"How did you—"

"Know?" She lifts her brows. "*I* remembered."

The corner of her lips twitch like she wants to laugh at her own joke, and part of me is dying to see it. In fact, I kind of want to see her *really* laugh, like throw her head back and just let it all out.

She punches my order into the tablet, then swings it around for me to pay. I make sure to tack on a twenty-dollar tip for the three-dollar coffee.

When she turns it back around, her eyes narrow on the screen for just a moment, but she doesn't say anything. Instead, she tucks her lips together and spins around to grab my drink.

"Busy today?" I ask her, flipping my hat around and leaning my arms against the truck.

I'm used to food trucks sitting high up off the ground, but she's lowered this one just a bit. I wonder if she did it to make it less intimidating for customers and kids.

"Yep."

That's all she says, but at least it's an answer, which is a hell of a lot more than I've gotten out of her in the last two weeks.

She turns around with my coffee in hand, securing my lid on the top before sliding it over to me. Then, she does what she usually does: ignores me.

She starts rearranging things, moving bowls around and stacking trays. I stand and watch the entire time, not saying a word.

As the seconds progress into minutes, her movements become more and more relaxed, like she's growing used to me standing there. I'm not sure if I should be flattered that she's feeling comfortable in my presence or offended that she's so easily able to pretend I don't exist.

A good five minutes pass before I start getting antsy and just *have* to say *something* to her.

"Got any plans for the rest of the day?"

She pauses, then peeks up at me.

Okay, she didn't jump, so maybe she *didn't* forget I was standing there.

"You're still here? I forgot all about you."

Ouch.

"Really? I thought you had such a good memory, though," I say, taking a sip of my coffee. It's scalding hot and tastes like someone bottled sadness and served it over hot coals. She must not miss my wince, because she holds her hand out for it. "What?"

"Your coffee. Hand it over."

I heed her command and slip the cup into her hand. She sets it to the side, then grabs one of the clear cups I've seen her use for iced coffees and grabs a pitcher from the fridge. She fills it about three-quarters of the way up, then dumps some ice into it before emptying one packet of sugar and adding a splash of milk to the mix. She caps the drink, gives it a shake, and hands it my way with a straw.

"Here. Try this."

Eying the cup with skepticism, I pull the straw from the wrapper and stick it into the lid, then take a small sip. And it's good—*so* much better than the hot coffee I've been drinking every time I come here.

"I notice you make a face every time you take a sip of your coffee." She shrugs. "I'm guessing you don't like hot coffee and cold brew might be more to your liking. The milk helps cut down on the bitterness that can occur."

I'm surprised. Coffee has never been my favorite thing to drink, but it gets the job done, so I always suffer through it. I've tried to doctor it up with the sugar and cinnamon, but it's never good. This may just be a game-changer for me.

"I take it you like it?" she asks after I've taken my second drink.

I nod. "It's good. No offense to whatever that other stuff was, but it's not for me."

"No offense taken. Not everyone likes hot coffee. I think it tastes like burnt water, but that's just me. Give me a vanilla cold brew any day of the week."

This is the most Scout's ever talked to me and certainly the most she's ever revealed about herself, though I'm not about to point that out because I'm terrified she'll stop talking to me again.

"Can I try the vanilla tomorrow?"

Just like that, her scowl slides back into place. "I thought you were joking about coming here and bothering me every day."

"Am I bothering you?"

She doesn't answer immediately like I expect her to. Instead, she chews on her bottom lip for a minute, contemplating that, likely wondering how honest she should be right now, eventually settling on a quiet, "No. You're not bothering me."

I grin, and her scowl deepens, causing me to laugh.

"Okay, *now* you're bothering me. Go away. I have to get ready for the lunch rush."

As she says this, two cars pull into the parking lot, and I know from experience that this place is about to be loaded with people looking for their midday caffeine fix and sugar high to get them through.

I shake my cup at her. "Thanks for this."

She nods but doesn't say anything else.

"I'll see you tomorrow, *friend*."

39

She grunts, and I laugh again.

"I'm going to wear you down, Scout. You're going to love me."

She scoffs and mutters something that sounds a lot like, "In your dreams, Miller."

I can't seem to wipe the smile off my face as I walk away.

CHAPTER 4

"Can I get a vanilla cold brew, please?" a voice says to my back.

I don't have to turn around to know it's Miller standing there. I can tell not only by his voice, which is so deep I swear he could narrate audiobooks, but by how my body seems to *know* when he's around.

I couldn't stop thinking about him after he left yesterday. Not even the lunch rush could distract me. All I could focus on was that he wasn't lying about returning. He showed up just like he said he would. Given that I thought this was all just a little game to him, it was surprising.

But today? Seeing him here yet again? That's even more of a shock.

I spin around to find him grinning at me with that same stupid smile he's always wearing and his whiskey eyes sparkling against the midday sun.

This is about the same time he showed up here yesterday, and I wonder if he's just getting out of practice. I know hockey season is right around the corner because my niece won't stop talking about it and how the Comets have a much better chance of not *Toronto-ing* this year, whatever the hell that means.

"Please?" he asks, and this time he actually bats his lashes at me…lashes that are thick and dark and frame his eyes perfectly.

For the first time in a long time, my fingers itch for a keyboard, because this right here is that moment in all novels where the guy walks up to the lonely, awkward girl and gives her that grin that makes her knees weak. I want to write a story about that grin.

Ugh, Scout! Stop thinking about how attractive he is. It's still the same guy who forgot who you were. He's just like everyone else.

I don't answer him. Instead, I ring up his coffee, then spin the tablet his way and get started on his drink. A slight sense of pride swells in my chest as I pour the cold brew and add a bit of vanilla syrup. I've been running this truck for a few years and have gotten good at reading customers. It didn't take me any time to realize Miller hates hot coffee. I wanted to say something about it to him before, but I've always been too nervous to approach him. Now, though, not so much.

He still makes me nervous, and my heart still feels like it wants to burst out of my chest, but he seems a little less scary than before.

I slide his coffee and straw across the counter, then flip the tablet back around. I can't help but frown at the number I see on the screen.

He tipped me big again.

I know I shouldn't be annoyed because hello, money! But still. It's like he's trying too hard to make up for forgetting me, which makes him showing up and bothering me feel like a show. A gimmick, like it's not genuine.

"You don't have to keep tipping me so big, you know. I already said I forgive you. No need to bribe me."

His lips pull down at the corners. "I'm not bribing you. I'm just grateful to now be drinking something I enjoy. Besides, I tip everyone big."

"Well, thanks," I murmur, a little annoyed at how flippantly he says that. I should have expected it, though. He's a famous hockey player; this is nothing to him.

"Thank *you*." He shakes his drink around, then takes another sip. "I really like the vanilla in this."

His compliment perks me up because I love when customers enjoy the things I make, especially the ones I work so hard on. "It's good, right? I made it."

"You made it?"

"Why are you surprised by that?"

"I...I don't know. I just figured it was bottled or something."

I shake my head. "Nope. Everything here is made fresh. Well, almost everything—I buy the sprinkles in bulk."

"Speaking of supplies..." He reaches into his back pocket and produces a little shaker of something. He sets it on the counter, then slides it my way. "For inventory."

I pick up the bottle of spice and can't help but laugh when I see what's on the label.

Nutmeg.

Just above it, he's scrawled *Scout's.*

"You got me my own nutmeg?"

He lifts a shoulder. "I heard you were running low. Didn't want you to run out. God forbid there's not enough for your Aww Nuts(meg) donut."

I grin, staring down at the bottle that I just know I'm never going to open. "Thanks. I'm sure my customers will appreciate it."

"Maybe I'm not so bad to have around, then, huh, *friend?*"

I roll my eyes. "No, you definitely are. Now, shoo. I apparently have some inventory to do before the lunch rush starts." I shake the bottle.

"Thanks again for this," he says, lifting his coffee before spinning on his heel.

"You're welcome," I mutter quietly to his retreating back.

I don't know how long I stand there and watch him walk away, but it's long enough for him to catch me staring and wink at me.

I scowl, and he laughs.

Then, I get to work.

"You have to fire her, Scout," Stevie says as she ties her hair up in a ponytail. "This is getting ridiculous. You can't keep covering for her. You're going to burn yourself out, then you'll never have time to get your book finished."

I let out a frustrated sigh as Stevie gives me the same speech she's been giving me for the last month.

She's right, but I don't want her to be right because that would mean I have to go through applications and all the hard work of finding another baker. I don't want to do that again, but I also don't want to spend every waking hour inside this truck. I love it, but I also love sliding into my bathtub with a bottle of wine and a good book on an off day, something I haven't had in far too long.

"I know, I know," I tell her as she wraps her apron around her waist and brushes past me, her lips set in a firm line. "It's just her dad is sick, and, well, I get it."

Stevie sends me a look as she passes by, a bowl of freshly made strawberry icing in hand. "That's bullshit, and you know it. Carla knows it too. Her dad had the *flu*. He's fine now. He's *been* fine. She's just taking advantage of you because she knows your history and because you're entirely too nice."

A part of me wants to believe Carla is a good person and she's not taking advantage of me, but I know Stevie is right. She *is* using my past against me and playing the sick dad card when I know for a fact he's fine. I saw him at the drugstore two days ago. He was in the hygiene aisle. I was grabbing tampons, and he was getting condoms. It's safe to say Carla's dad is hunky-dory.

"Did I just hear you say Scout is nice?" My skin instantly buzzes at the sound of Miller's voice. "Because if so, why has she never shown that side of herself to me?"

I turn around to find the hockey player who just won't go away standing at the front of the truck with a playful sparkle in his eyes. He's been here every day for the last week, and I'm really starting to wonder when he's going to get tired of this game and finally leave me alone.

Right now, it doesn't look like it'll be anytime soon.

Stevie tilts her head at me, likely waiting for me to run away or duck down and hide. When I don't, her brows rise in a way that says we'll definitely be discussing this later.

I *really* don't want to discuss it later.

In fact, I was *really* hoping Miller wouldn't even show today.

But, of course, he did.

And now he *and* my sister are looking at me expectantly.

With a sigh, I wave a hand toward him. "Miller, meet my older sister, Stevie. Stevie, this is Miller. He plays—"

"Right wing. He had 90 points last year and was ranked one of the top eight forwards in the league by *SportsCenter.*" She wipes her hand on her apron, then extends it his way. "I know who you are, Mr. Miller. My daughter won't stop talking about the Comets. She's a huge fan."

Miller grins, then slides his hand against hers. "Grady is fine. And I love hearing that. It's always nice to meet a fan."

Oh, he has his charm turned all the way up today. I can tell by the way he's smiling at her and puffing his chest out just a bit.

"I'm not a fan. My daughter is."

I can't help but laugh when Stevie kills his ego with a few simple words.

"I mean, don't get me wrong, I'm a huge Comets fan, but Beast is my favorite player by far."

"That grump?" Miller scoffs. "I'm way better than Rhodes."

"Keep telling yourself that," Stevie tells him. "So, did you finally apologize to my sister for being an ass?"

Miller's gaze snaps to mine, and my whole system goes into shock because there's no way she actually just said that, knowing full well that it implies...

"You've been talking about me?" Miller says with a cocky smile. "I knew you liked me, Scout."

I roll my eyes. "I liked you better when you didn't know who I was."

He just laughs as I turn to make his coffee for him. I contemplate screwing it up to get back at him for embarrassing me just now, but I can't bring myself to mess with a customer's order—no matter how annoying they are.

When I slide the finished drink his way, he's still grinning, and when I see the total on the screen, I know why. He left me another twenty-dollar tip. It makes me want to reach across the counter and wipe the smug smirk from his face.

"Stop it," I grumble, and all he does is laugh.

"Don't worry, I won't tease you about it too much. I knew all along there was no way you could actually hate me. I'm impossible to hate."

"I don't think that's the case at all."

"Pretty sure it is," he argues, taking a drink of his coffee. "Ah, just the way I like it. Only a *friend* would remember that."

Stevie points from me to Miller. "You two are friends now?"

"No." Miller shakes his head. "Can you believe your sister won't be friends with me?"

"With as charming as you are, I'm shocked," she quips.

"Right?" Miller says, not knowing Stevie well enough to understand she's definitely making fun of him right now. "She doesn't know what she's missing—I'm a great friend."

Stevie looks up from the concoction she's currently working on, quirking a brow at me. There are a million questions she's asking me in that single movement. I shake my head as subtly as I can, telling her we'll discuss it later...if she can find me, that is. I have big plans to run and hide and avoid her forever because I do not want to get in to whatever it is Miller is doing since I'm not sure how I feel about it yet. He's shown up every day, and I really don't know what that means or what I want it to mean.

"What's that you're making?" Miller asks, nodding toward the bowl of vanilla frosting I'm currently folding quins sprinkles into.

"It's filling."

"A new donut?"

"Sort of. It was here in June, but I decided to keep it as a full-time item, and I'll be adding it starting tomorrow. We're doing a little promo thing for it."

"What is it?"

"It's a Pride donut. We're calling it Live Out Proud."

"Sweet. *Literally.*" He looks mighty proud of himself for the pun.

"It's for our dads," Stevie tells him. "Scout always wanted to make a donut that celebrated their love, and she finally perfected it this summer, so now it's going to be a regular menu item."

"That's awesome. I bet they're ridiculously proud of you. Are they hockey fans? If so, I'll gladly bring some jerseys or pucks next time I stop by."

Stevie's gaze catches mine for only a moment before she says, "Oh, well, Dad wasn't always but is now. Pops, on the other hand—"

"I think your phone is buzzing," I cut her off.

I feel bad because her phone didn't really buzz, but just like I knew it would, it draws her attention and sends her rushing toward the other end of the truck where she keeps her purse just in case it has something to do with Macie.

Miller tips his head, watching me expectantly like I'm going to finish where Stevie left off, but I'm not. I don't want her spilling our personal details to him, so I'm not about to either, especially when I'm still not sure what his endgame is here.

I ignore him and continue mixing the sprinkles and the frosting. I'm sure it's plenty combined by now, but I don't want to not have anything to do with my hands, not with him standing there with that damn cold brew and those damn watchful eyes.

"Oh, I'm all good. It wasn't mine," Stevie says, pocketing her phone and coming back to the front. "Maybe it was yours? It could be Carla ready to come and actually do her job for once."

"Who's Carla?" Miller asks.

"My other baker," I answer, and Stevie huffs. I shoot her a glare, though she doesn't see it because she's back to working on her own project. "She called in today."

"And every other day she was scheduled this week for absolutely no reason."

Another glare Stevie's way.

Miller's face goes from carefree to cloudy in a split second, like *he's* the one angry about Carla not showing up. "That's bullshit, Scout. You shouldn't let her use you like that. Hell, you shouldn't let *anyone* use you. You're worth more than that. You should talk with her, lay down the ground rules. And if she gives you shit, fire her. You'll find someone better—someone who values your time and your business the way you do. That's what you deserve."

His tone...the way he sounds like he's talking from experience...it has a lump forming in my throat because I was not expecting that. I'm used to lectures from Stevie, but this? This felt different.

I find myself nodding and saying, "Okay." Mostly because I'm not entirely sure how I'm supposed to respond. "I'll talk to her."

"Good." He nods, seemingly satisfied with my answer. He lifts his drink. "Thank you for the coffee." He looks to Stevie. "It was great to officially meet you. Let me know if your dads ever want anything. I'm happy to bring it by."

"I will," Stevie promises, a sad smile on her face that Miller definitely doesn't pick up on. "Nice meeting you, Grady."

He turns his attention to me, and I swear my body hums from the way his eyes bore into mine. "I'll see you soon, *friend*."

"Goodbye, Miller." This time, the eye roll I give him comes a little more reluctantly, but it doesn't bother him either way. He just sends me that same charming smile before heading for his car, and I watch him walk away yet again.

Stevie watches too, only it's not him she's looking at. It's me.

Her stare is burning a hole in the side of my head. I

can practically hear the hundreds of questions she's hurling my way without saying a word.

Unable to take it anymore, I finally say, "Just say whatever it is you're going to say."

"I was just going to say that I like him. He seems nice."

I huff out a laugh, dragging my eyes away from Miller as he climbs into his fancy-pants sports car that probably costs more than I make in a year. "Don't forget that he forgot who I was just three weeks ago."

"I didn't forget, but he seems determined to make up for it."

"He's trying too hard."

"Or…" She stretches the word out. "He's just a really nice person who made a mistake, and we shouldn't judge him. You're willing to give Carla all the room in the world to make mistake after mistake, but not Grady? Why is that?"

Because Carla can't hurt me like Miller can.

I don't say it out loud. I don't have to. Stevie knows my reasons for keeping Miller at arm's length.

"He could be good for you, Scout. He could get you out of this truck and out of the apartment. He could be a good inspiration for the novel you still haven't finished."

Or started. But I don't tell her that.

The last time I touched the book I promised I'd write was three years ago, and that was to delete it. Every time I've sat down to write since then, the words won't come, which really sucks for someone who wants so badly to be published.

I know the reason I can't write. I know the reason my mind is all blocked. I'm lacking inspiration, lacking excitement.

I need both badly.

I'm just not so sure I'm ready, especially if it means that inspiration and excitement come in the form of Grady Miller.

He's a hotshot hockey player, and I'm not sure I want to play his game.

CHAPTER 5

"Did you get my texts last night?"

I look up to find Greer standing over me while I'm holding a hundred and twenty-five pounds over my head. "I did."

"And?" he presses, eyebrow raised.

At nearly midnight, my phone started blowing up with photos from Greer. They were all of women he thought I could get to be my date for the fundraiser. They were hot, I'll give him that, but blind dates— especially from Greer—aren't really my thing. If I'm going to be stuck at this damn function all night, I want to be stuck with someone I'm actually going to enjoy spending time with. Besides, I'm not in a huge rush. I still have time to find a date.

"And no," I tell him, shoving the weights back up and setting the bar on the rack. I sit up, sucking in a much-needed breath of air. I reach for the towel that's on the bench next to me and wipe my face down. "I appreciate the thought, but I'm like ninety percent sure I saw you making out with one of them at Slapshots last month, and I'm not really into dating my teammate's seconds."

"Your loss." Greer shrugs. "She's a great kisser."

"Duly noted."

"And I know she'd take care of your…issue for you."

I know exactly what he's referring to: my virginity.

"I'm good," I tell him, trying not to get irritated. "And I thought we talked about how I don't want or need your help."

He shrugs, then taps my shoulder, wanting my spot. I get up and move to the front of the bench to spot him as he picks the bar up and lifts it off the rack. He shoves the bar up easily, going slow and doing measured reps.

"I have a few other options lined up if you need 'em." He presses the weight away from his chest again. "And if all else fails, you can always take your mom. I know the new rookie is doing that."

I inwardly groan at the idea of going to any sort of public event with my mother. Sure, my dad was hardest on me growing up when it came to hockey, but my mother was tough on me in other areas. Her favorite thing to do was chastise me for the smallest of mistakes any time we left the house. My shoes were too scuffed or my shirt wasn't tucked in correctly or my hair was out of place. It wouldn't matter if I spent an hour getting ready for dinner out at the local Dairy Queen—it was never enough.

I couldn't even begin to imagine what it would be like to take her to the fundraiser.

"I'd rather ask Wright's mother-in-law."

"Hey! Leave her out of this, Miller! Swear to God, I will chop your dick off if I catch you flirting with her again!" Wright shouts from a few rows down as he pedals hard on the stationary bike.

I laugh, truly enjoying fucking with him. Don't get me wrong, his mother-in-law is gorgeous, and I love flirting with her because it makes her feel good, but it's all in good fun. Truth is, I just like spending time around her because she's the kind of mother I wish I had—warm, thoughtful, and kind.

"There's always Ryan's grandma," Lowell offers up. "You know Grams will take you up on that offer. I'm pretty sure she's still swooning over your moves at Wright's wedding."

Rhodes is grumbling and throwing warning glances my way before Lowell even gets his whole sentence out.

Okay, so maybe I don't have the best track record when it comes to flirting with the older women in my teammates' lives. What can I say? It's fun to mess with them. They make it entirely too easy.

"I'll keep her in mind," I say just to fuck with Rhodes, who smashes the off button on his treadmill, then marches out of the room in a grumpy huff.

Greer laughs as he sets the bar back on the rack and sits up. "You're just asking to get your ass handed to you out on the ice. You know that, right?"

I shrug. "Eh. I can take him."

"You can take Beast? Even I wouldn't fuck with him."

I lean down and not-so-quietly say, "Don't let him fool you. He's just a big ol' softy underneath all that hard exterior."

"I heard you, you little shit!" Rhodes yells from the adjoining room. "I'll fucking show you softy," he mutters, and I'd bet my left nut he's scowling like crazy right now.

I laugh, then move over to the stationary bike next to Wright.

"You having trouble finding a date for the fundraiser? Mr. Casanova himself? Dry spell?"

Ha. If he only knew.

"Something like that," I say just to get him off my back.

Wright chuckles. "I'd offer one of Harper's friends, but, well, she's a complete introvert, and her only friend is Ryan. I don't think Rhodes would take too kindly to that."

"Come near her and die," Rhodes threatens, walking by and making sure to hit me with his bag.

I laugh as he makes his way out of the training room, flipping everyone off behind his back, likely running right back home to his wife and locking her away in his big dark castle so no one else can come near her.

I'd think it was sweet if I wasn't so damn jealous of him.

"Well, you better get out of whatever rut you're in because I'm pretty sure Coach will have our asses if anyone shows up dateless. Then we'd have to worry about Smith, too, because this is his passion project he's heading this year."

"I know, I know," I grumble. "I've got it taken care of."

Except I don't have it taken care of, not even a little bit.

I am so screwed.

Something is wrong.

It's the first thought that runs through my head when I pull into the parking lot of Scout's Sweets. The line is snaked through the tables, so long it almost touches said lot, which is overflowing. All eight tables are decorated with bundles of balloons and completely full of customers. There's music playing over a few speakers that are set up where there's typically a little library for browsing.

There are a few patrons who appear annoyed, but for the most part, people are smiling, which I suppose is a good thing. Still, this line isn't normal. There has to be a reason it's backed up so much.

I grab my ballcap and tug it low over my head, then make my way toward the front of the truck. A few people throw me curious glances, but nobody says anything, and I'm glad because I am clearly skipping the line.

When I get about twenty feet away, I see what the problem is: Scout is alone, and she's struggling to keep up with the line.

Her hair, which is usually a bit of a mess anyway, is even more chaotic. Her apron is covered in what I assume is flour. There's a streak of it on her cheek. Her eyes are wide yet tired somehow, but even though she's having trouble, she's wearing a smile and greeting customers like a champ.

I'm not surprised when her gaze finds me standing off to the side.

Fuck. She looks worse than I thought, like she's barely hanging on by a thread, and I hate it so much. Her eyes begin to glisten, and it seems like she's only a few moments away from breaking down completely.

She shakes her head and mouths, *Go.*

I don't.

In fact, I walk closer. I don't stop until I'm waltzing into the truck like I own the place. I grab the other apron hanging on the hook and slide it over my head. Then, I spin my cap around and look at her.

"Put me to work."

"Miller, I don't have time for this today. I have——"

"Put. Me. To. Work," I repeat.

Her eyes widen at the sternness in my voice, but to my surprise, she doesn't argue. Instead, she reaches out and grabs a fistful of my shirt, yanking me closer to her. She pulls me in front of the register and points at it.

"You take orders, I'll fill them. If they order a simple coffee, make it. Leave the complex ones to me. Make sure to hand them a straw if they order an iced coffee."

"I got this," I promise, even though I have no clue at all how to work any of the machines. "Go." I wave her off, then shoot a big smile at the customer standing in front of me. "Welcome to Scout's Sweets, the best damn donuts in the city. What can I get for you today?"

I swear I see her shoulders sag in relief in my periphery, but I refuse to look at her.

"Hey, can I get a half dozen Live Out Proud donuts?"

Oh crap, that's right—she's debuting her new donut. No wonder this place is packed.

"Sure thing," I say, searching for the donut on the tablet and trying to figure out how to ring up a half dozen. "Just one second..." I mutter.

"Take your time, man," the guy says. "None of us mind waiting. We're all here to celebrate Scout for being so damn amazing. We can wait a few minutes, right, everyone?" he says loudly, addressing the crowd.

Multiple people throw their arms up and whoop loudly, cheering Scout on.

I love it for her, and I'm a little mad at myself for not seeing how amazing she is before.

"She's thankful you all showed up today. Should have seen her gushing about these donuts yesterday," I tell him, finally finding the button on the screen. I swing the machine over his way like I've seen Scout do so many times before. "They're for her dads, which I think is pretty cool."

He smiles up at me, pays, then steps off to the side to wait.

"Next!" I call out.

And that's how the next several hours go. The line is crazy and seems never-ending, but when three o'clock rolls around, it finally dwindles until we only have a handful of customers left, and I've never been happier. I've had to sit through many autograph lines in my career, but never anything like this. I don't know how Scout's doing it because she hasn't taken a break once since I got here, and there's no telling the last time she actually had one.

"Hey," I say gently, placing a hand on her shoulder and stepping up behind her.

She freezes for a moment before she realizes it's me, then relaxes into my touch. I think it's a good thing I'm standing so close to her because I swear she's about to collapse into my arms. I'd catch her too.

"Take a break," I tell her softly.

"Huh?" She seems dazed, like she's working on pure instinct right now. I honestly don't think she even knows what she's doing anymore.

"A break—you need one. Take it. I can handle the rest of these customers."

Her brows are crushed together when she finally

spins around. I try my hardest to ignore how close we're currently standing, but it's hard because she's right there. We've never been this close before…and I don't hate it.

If she notices this too, she doesn't say anything.

"Let me take care of this," I insist. "Go relax."

She traps her bottom lip between her teeth, chewing on it as she considers my offer. She's tired. She knows she's tired, but she's scared to leave her baby in my hands.

It feels like forever before she finally nods and agrees to go. She unties her apron from around her waist and slips it over her head. She makes herself a fresh coffee, then disappears around the back side of the truck.

I take care of the last few people in line, then get to work on cleaning the truck the best I can. It's a mess, but I'm sure once Scout sees how much she's made today in tips alone, it'll all be worth it.

I laugh when I slide a bottle of nutmeg onto the shelf, noting the other three bulk-size containers there. When I'm finished, I go looking for Scout.

I find her completely deflated, sitting hunched over in a fold-out lawn chair. I've never been back here before, but it's clear she uses this area for her breaks.

She looks exhausted, like she could sleep for the next twelve hours and still not be rested. I approach slowly, dropping down into the chair beside her.

She perks up when she hears it squeak and starts to stand, but I grab her wrist to stop her.

"No. Rest."

"But the truck…"

"Is fine. I put the *Be Right Back* sign up. We have fifteen minutes."

"Yeah, but did you—"

"Lock down the register? Yes. It's all good." I don't tell her I know how to lock it down because I accidentally did it earlier and spent five minutes figuring out how to get back into it. She should change her passcode to something other than *donuts*.

"Oh." She drops back into her chair. "Okay."

We sit in silence for several minutes, both of us just trying to relax for the first time in hours.

"That was…"

"Absolute chaos?" she finishes with a sardonic laugh.

"Yeah. I don't know how you do that regularly."

"It's normally not so bad. I usually have help, but…"

"Carla?" I guess. She nods. "Fucking Carla."

"When I texted her last night, she swore she would be in today for the launch, but guess who didn't show when I was here to prep at five?"

"Fucking Carla?"

"Yep. So, I fired her, because you were right—I'm worth more than the bullshit she was slinging my way."

I grin. "Say that again."

"I'm worth more than—"

"You are, but not that part. The other one."

She peeks over at me, head tilted. Then she realizes

what I'm asking, and she laughs. Only this time, it's not sarcastic or mean. It's genuine.

"You were right, Miller."

"Ah," I say, stretching my legs out and folding my hands over my stomach. "I love it when you say sweet things to me."

She rolls her eyes, but I don't miss the way her lips tip up into a grin.

"I'm sorry she bailed on you. Was Stevie not available?"

"No. She had a thing at Macie's school. She helps out there a few times a week. I couldn't ask her to ditch that for my little donut truck."

I don't like the way she says *little donut truck*, like this doesn't matter or something, but she's tired and worn out, so I don't say anything.

"I guess I'm going to have to hire someone else." She groans, sitting forward and dropping her head into her hands. "Ugh. I've done so well not thinking about it all day, and now I am and—"

"Did you know a blue whale's dick is massive? We're talking eight to ten feet easily."

Her mouth hangs open as she stares at me in complete shock. After several seconds, she shakes her head. "I... I... What the hell, Miller?"

I laugh. "Got you to stop thinking about Fucking Carla, didn't it?"

Slowly, her look of shock transforms into a soft smile, and I realize then that I like her smile. A lot.

She settles back into her chair, looking a lot less stressed.

"Thank you," she says quietly after a few silent moments. "For today. You have no idea how much I appreciate it."

"It's nothing," I tell her with a shrug. "Besides, that's what *friends* are for, right?"

She rolls her head my way, that same smile still playing on her lips. "Yeah, I guess so... *friend*."

"Holy shit!" I holler, jumping out of my chair. "You just called me your friend!"

"Ugh." She grumbles again, rising to her feet. "Don't make me take it back already."

"You can't. No takesies-backsies."

"Oh, I can definitely take it back." She points at me as she passes. "And I will, so behave."

I hold my hands up, trailing behind her as we head back, our fifteen minutes up. "Yes, ma'am."

We clamber back into the truck, and her eyes widen in surprise when she takes in the state of things.

"Miller..." She says my name softly, like a prayer. "You cleaned up?"

"Best as I could. I wasn't sure where to put some things, so I left those out."

"This is a million times better than it was."

I shrug, not telling her I'm kind of a neat freak thanks to all my years having to pretend to have the perfect family. When you have a family like mine, you get good

65

at cleaning up messes and making things look put together real fast.

"You really didn't have to do all this, but I appreciate it so much. I don't know what I would have done without you today."

I'm not sure why, but her words strike me right in the chest and settle. They burrow into the cavity and latch onto something deep inside of me.

"It was nothing."

She pins me with a stare that says she knows I'm lying. I'm a fucking pro hockey player whose season is careening closer every day; it's not like I don't have things to do. I'm supposed to be training. I'm supposed to be finishing up paperwork. I have homework, like watching tapes and getting ready for a grueling six-plus months ahead of me.

But she lets me have the words anyway and begins cleaning up the rest of the supplies, dropping them into the sink with a promise to clean them later. We work side by side, picking up the truck and packing away some leftovers she's sure she won't be able to sell today.

"Well fucking well," a voice calls from out front. It's followed by a low whistle and a laugh. "I didn't expect to find you here."

Shit.

I peek up from the donuts I'm currently boxing up to find Greer grinning at me smugly.

"Hey," I say like an idiot.

He laughs. "Hey? *Hey?* That's all I get? Especially when you're here with donut girl?"

"Her name's Scout."

"Oh, good. You remembered," the woman in question says, sliding up next to me. "Not sure we've officially been introduced." I've been on the receiving end of her icy stares enough times to know that's what she's sending Greer's way right now. She looks polite and sweet, but the look she's giving him is anything but.

"Greer."

"Do you work with Miller or something?"

He lifts a brow, his jaw tightening when she doesn't recognize him. His ego is big enough that it annoys him, but it entertains me.

"Or something," he mutters, then looks at me. "You get the group text?"

I know which one he's referring to without asking. It was a chain put together by Smith when he retired that includes him, me, Wright, Rhodes, Lowell, and Greer. We have a strict no-work-talk policy in place. It's just a place for us to shoot the shit and keep in touch.

I pull my phone out of my pocket, surprised to find a ton of unanswered texts. I've been ignoring it all day, and now I wish I hadn't.

Smith: I'm saying this as your friend, but I swear, if any of you show up without dates, I'll make you skate circles for shits and giggles.

. . .

Wright: As your friend…fuck off. You're not even our real coach, old man.

Smith: Am too!

Wright: Whatever you say, Apple.

Rhodes: You do realize most of the guys in this chat are married, right?

Lowell: I'm not married.

Wright: No, but you're stupidly in love with your baby momma.

Lowell: Damn right I am.

Rhodes: Aw, he's finally found his feelings. How sweet.

. . .

Wright: Like you're one to talk, Beast.

Rhodes: *middle-finger emoji*

Smith: What? No comments from the rookie?

Lowell: He's not a rookie anymore. We're not allowed to call him that. We gotta get a better nickname for him.

Rhodes: How about little shithead?

Wright: Or numbnuts?

Lowell: Come on, guys…

Wright: You ruin all the fun, Captain.

Rhodes: Yeah, who else are we supposed to make fun of? Greer?

· · ·

Greer: Go for it. I have no feelings.

Greer: And don't worry, I have a date lined up. Can't speak for Miller, though.

Smith: Dammit. Someone get the kid on board.

Greer: Whatever you say, Gramps.

Smith: *middle-finger emoji*

With a groan, I shove the phone back into my pocket.

Scout wasn't the only one who used today as a distraction from her issues. The guys have been on my ass all week about getting a date for the fundraiser. I'm down to just two weeks to find someone, and my options still aren't looking good. To be fair, I haven't been spending any time looking either.

"So, have you found a date yet?" Greer asks. "Or do you need help considering your…" He flicks his eyes to Scout. "*Issue.*"

Fuck. I haven't, and he knows I haven't, which is going to make this ten times more embarrassing to say in front of Scout.

"I—"

"You didn't tell him, Miller?" Scout says, bumping my shoulder playfully and giving a flirty smirk, a far cry from how she normally is with me. Then she looks at Greer. "I'm his date."

CHAPTER 6

SCOUT

"I'm his date."

What the fuck, Scout?! What are you doing?

Greer looks from me to Miller and back to me again. It's clear he's sizing us up, trying to decide if he's going to believe us or not.

I hope he does because being embarrassed by two different hockey players in one month would be truly traumatizing.

After a few moments, a smile spreads across his face. "Well, smack my ass." He shakes his head. "Didn't expect that one, but I'm happy all the same. Smith will be too."

"Smith?" I question.

"Yeah, he's heading the fundraiser you're my *date* for," Miller says, widening his eyes at me, encouraging me to play along.

"Oh, yeah." I nod. "That's right. You told me that. Duh." I smack my forehead. I force a grin Greer's way. "Sorry, long day. Speaking of…can I get you anything?"

"An iced coffee would be great. Black, please."

I scurry away to fulfill his request but keep my ears tuned in to the conversation they begin to mutedly have the moment my back is turned.

"When the hell did this happen?" Greer asks. "And how? I thought she hated you."

"I'm charming," Miller insists, and I can just picture him grinning like a fool.

"You're an idiot, and we both know it. You're not paying her, are you?"

I'm insulted by that accusation for myself *and* for Miller. Is he really insinuating that Miller would have to pay someone to date him? He's a damn hockey player! There is no way women aren't falling at his feet. Or skates. Whatever.

"No, asshole. This is completely consensual. Trust me, I was just as surprised by it as you are."

I tuck my lips together, trying not to laugh because, for once, he's not lying. I have no idea why I said I was his date. I don't even know what I'm his date for. I also have no idea what *issue* he was referring to—though that part does have me curious— but I'm not going to let Miller be picked on by his teammate.

"You swear you're not coercing her?"

"I swear to God, Greer, I will nail your nuts to the locker room benches if you insult me again. I'll—"

"Here's that coffee," I say, spinning back around, cutting off whatever threat was going to tumble from Miller's mouth next—not because I'm worried for Greer, but mostly because I find it insanely hot to see Miller get all worked up.

They break apart, and Greer shoots me a grin I suppose is meant to be charming but is nothing like the ones Miller throws my way. There's nothing genuine about it.

"Thanks," he mutters, taking a sip, eying his teammate the whole time. They're having a silent conversation now, much like the ones Stevie and I have. I'd kill to know what they're saying. "So, what happened here today? How'd you rope Miller into getting behind the register?"

"I didn't. He volunteered."

Greer's brows shoot up at that. "Interesting."

"Not really," Miller mumbles. "Is that all you stopped by for? Coffee?"

His teammate laughs at his obvious annoyance. "Yep." He takes another sip, then smacks his lips. "Ahh. Refreshing."

"Oh my god!"

A distant voice calls out, and we all turn our attention to find Stevie practically dragging my niece behind her as they hustle toward the truck.

When she approaches, she takes in the messy picnic tables and the trash cans that desperately need to be emptied and winces. "I am *so* sorry, Scout. I couldn't bail on Macie, though. I—"

I hold my hand up, stopping her. "It's fine. Macie comes first. I understand."

I look over the edge of the truck and wave down at my niece, but she's not paying me any attention.

Instead, she's looking up at Greer, her brows slammed down tight, scowling up at him. I want to chastise her for being impolite, but then I notice what Greer's doing…he's scowling at her too.

"You're tall," she tells him.

"You're short," he shoots back with just as much sass as she's throwing his way.

She curls her lips back at him, and he does the same. It's comical watching a grown man sneering at a little girl.

Macie being Macie, she crosses her arms over her chest and doesn't back down. "Are you going to win us a Cup this year? Because if not, I'm sure Johnson can step in as goalie."

Miller lets out a low laugh, and Macie turns her fiery gaze his way.

"Your shots on goal were down last season, you know. You have no room to be laughing at him."

"Yes, ma'am," he says, and I swear he stands up straighter as if afraid of the nine-year-old.

Not that I'd entirely blame him. Macie can be quite scary at times. She's got fire, that's for sure.

"Macie May, you're being rude."

She puffs her chest out. "I'm being tough, like Coach Heller. One day, when I'm an NHL coach, my team is going to win just like this team will. Just wait and see."

I love that she's already planning to infiltrate a male-dominated industry. Hell, I just might believe she could do it too.

"*You're* going to be a coach?" Greer challenges. "How about you get all your teeth before you start bossing people around, huh?"

Her stare could make grown men crumble to their knees.

But not Greer.

He just laughs, which fires her up even more. I feel like she's about two seconds away from hauling off and kicking the guy when Stevie steps up to him.

"How about you stop picking on a little kid and maybe stop a puck or two, goalie?"

Greer's eyes darken at her words, and a muscle begins to throb in his jaw. "That so?"

"Yep," Stevie says, not backing down. It's where Macie gets her spark from. My sister is one of the strongest women I know. She's been through a lot, and I know she makes sure her kid is strong because of it. "That's so."

"Hmph." Greer makes a non-committal noise, then turns to Miller. "Don't forget to let Smith know about your...*date*."

Stevie's head whips my way, and I do my best to ignore the stare she's sending me. I already know we're going to be discussing this later, even though I have no clue what to tell her other than I've clearly lost my mind.

"Bye, Twerp," he says to Macie.

She bares her teeth at him, staring him down until

he's in the parking lot, then she hitches her thumb over her shoulder toward him and says, "What's up his ass?"

"Macie!" Stevie admonishes.

"What? You said I could say ass sometimes!"

"I said you could say *jackass*."

"Fine. Then what's up his *jack*ass?"

"Oh my god. I swear, kid..." Stevie hangs her head, trying not to laugh. "Come on," she says, nudging Macie. "Let's go clean these tables up for Auntie Scout." Stevie gives me a pointed look that says *We'll talk about this later,* then begins picking up the mess the customers left behind.

When she and Macie are out of earshot, Miller turns to me.

"You can bail, you know. You didn't have to do that and save me in front of Greer." He drags his hand over the back of his neck, something I've noticed him do before. I wonder if it's a nervous thing. "You don't even know what it's for, and I know you probably don't want to spend time with me, and that's fine. I get it, so you're good. We're good. You don't have to go."

"Are you finished?" I ask when he's done rambling on.

He tips his head to the side. "Yes?"

"Good. Now, hush and tell me the details. I'm going to need to wear a fancy dress, I assume."

"You're..." His tongue darts out to wet his bottom lip. "You're going? Are you sure?"

I lift a shoulder. "Sure. Why not? You bailed me out

big-time today. I figure I owe you one. I'll be your date, Miller—but as friends, nothing else."

A slow, satisfied smile stretches across his face, and I have to fight back my own grin.

"Friends, huh?" he asks.

"Friends." He fist-pumps the air several times, and I point at him. "Don't make me regret this."

"Me? Never."

Then he winks.

And I swear my crush grows just a little stronger.

"Please tell me this isn't a joke and you actually are meeting *the* Grady Miller for a date?"

I sigh, pulling a shirt off the hanger. "It's not a date. We're just going shopping."

"Right. For your *date*."

I slip the mustard yellow t-shirt over my head, hiding my eye roll. It's been four days since the Donut Day from Hell, and I still can't believe I, Scout Thomas, made plans with Miller to go shopping.

Apparently, this event I'm attending with him is for a fundraiser that's helping raise money to get hockey equipment and practice space for underprivileged areas. It brings in a lot of cash for a good cause sponsored by professional athletes, which means there are going to be a buttload of photographers there. Those were Miller's words, not mine.

So, we're dress shopping.

I told him I could find something to wear on my own just fine, but he refused to take no for an answer, insisting he was paying for the dress. Who am I to pass up free clothes?

Stevie throws herself back on my bed with a dreamy sigh. "My sister, dating a hockey star...who would have thought?"

"For the billionth time, we aren't dating. It is *one* date, and it's for charity, which means it doesn't even count."

"Yeah, but it could be the start of something."

I bark out a laugh. "Ha. Not happening."

"Why not?" She rolls onto her stomach and kicks her feet back and forth, watching as I yank and pull my jeans over my wide hips. "He's not—"

"I know he's not," I cut her off. "But it's not going to happen, so just drop it."

She lifts her brows at my stern words. "Can I just say one last thing?"

I groan, knowing she's not going to let it go. She never does, so I motion for her to speak.

"He's nice." I open my mouth to argue, but she holds her hand up. "Aside from that one stupid thing he did, he seems like a really good guy. He helped you run your truck. He—an actual NHL player—helped you run your truck when I'm sure he has a million other things to do. *That* is nice."

I try to speak again, but she beats me to it.

"On top of all that...you like him. Hell, you've been

crushing on him for like two years now. And sure, I know it's mostly innocent, but why does it have to be? If he's interested in you, go for it. He makes you smile. He makes you laugh. And honestly…" She looks pointedly at the stacks of romance novels scattered throughout my room. "You need a little something in your life to shake things up. You can't hide forever."

I follow her gaze, trying to see what my room looks like through her eyes. Probably sad and lonely and boring, even though it's not.

I'm not ashamed of my reading habits. Hell, I could have much worse hobbies. But I also know at some point, I have to stop hiding behind the pages of a book and actually live, which is what she's getting at.

I want to. I really do.

But I'm also scared.

What if I get hurt? I've had my heart crushed enough in my short life. I don't want it obliterated again.

Also, if I'm not out living life and trying new things, how am I ever going to really be able to write a book about an epic romance? I mean, sure, there's my imagination and all that, but sometimes that real-life epic experience makes it all that much more believable. I follow all of my favorite romance authors on social media, and they're always posting about how funny or hot or charming their husbands are, how they met in the sweetest ways, how they're soulmates.

I want that *and* I want the career.

I love baking and making donuts, but I love love just a

little more, especially after witnessing what my dads had together.

"I know," I mutter. "I know. I'll work on it."

"And if by chance at the end of your date he asks you on another, you'll say yes?" She bats her lashes at me.

I laugh. Like legit laugh out loud.

Miller being interested in me? Yeah right.

"That's not going to happen."

"It could."

"It won't, Stevie. You're nuts."

"Am not! In fact, I'm so sure it will happen because I have eyes, and I've seen the way that boy looks at you. I want you to pinky swear that if he asks you out, you'll say yes."

"Fine." I cross the room, hooking my little finger with her outstretched one. "I pinky swear. But I'm only doing this because I know for a fact it'll never happen."

"Uh-huh." She smiles smugly. "We'll see about that."

I refused to give Miller my address.

Not because I don't trust him, but because I didn't want him to see my apartment. He's a multi-millionaire, for crying out loud. The last thing he needs to see is that I live with my sister and her daughter.

So, I made him meet me at the donut truck.

He's already waiting for me when I pull my trusty old

Toyota into the lot. It's almost comical when I park it next to his very expensive, very luxurious car.

I do one last mirror check to make sure I didn't sweat off all my makeup on the drive over, then shut off my car and hop out.

"Hi, friend," he says, pushing off the back of his vehicle.

"Miller," I respond coolly.

He chuckles. "You ready?"

"As I'll ever be."

I'm shocked when he follows me to the passenger side and pulls my door open for me.

"What?" he asks when I peek up at him. "I'm a gentleman."

"That is not a word I would use to describe you."

"Which word would you use, then?"

"Annoying. Irritating. Obnoxious. An absolute pain in my ass."

"That's six words."

"Huh?"

"An absolute pain in my ass—that's six words."

"Point proven," I say, sliding past him and into the car.

The minute I settle in, I'm assaulted by the scent that's all Miller. It's woodsy with just a hint of something else I can't quite place. It's intoxicating.

"Are you sniffing my car?"

I startle, because I didn't even realize he'd already gotten in.

"Uh…yes?"

His lips twitch, but he lets it go. "You okay with stopping and grabbing some coffee? I'm exhausted after practice."

"Oh, I could run into the truck and get us some if you want." I grab the handle, but he wraps his hand around my other wrist, stopping me. His touch is like a warm blanket on a cool autumn night, and I swear I feel it down to my toes.

"No," he says. "Today is your day off. Enjoy it."

"It's just coffee…"

He shakes his head. "Nope. You need to get out of that truck. No working today, got it?"

I find myself nodding, agreeing to the demand he has no business making. "Okay."

"Good." He removes his hand, and I instantly feel cold.

Then he smiles, and that same heat is back.

No—it's worse than before. I don't feel it in my toes; I feel it between my legs.

I swallow down the lump forming in my throat and force a smile of my own. "So, where to?"

"Figured we'd stop by Cup of Joe's and then hit up Julia's?"

"That shop downtown?" He nods, and I laugh. "Yeah, no. They are not going to have my size there."

His brows squeeze together. "Why not?"

I wave a hand over my body. "Because I'm not exactly small, Miller. I have big hips. I have an even bigger ass. I have stomach rolls that aren't so keen on being squeezed into tight dresses. I'm not a walk-into-any-store-and-find-a-dress kind of girl, and we don't have time to order something."

"Yeah, but—"

I shake my head, cutting him off. "No. I know a place where we can go."

"Are you sure?"

"Yup." I clap my hands together. "Chop-chop. We don't have all the time in the world. We have a deadline with this."

He sends me one last long glance but puts the car into drive.

If I thought Miller's driving was erratic as a bystander, it's nothing compared to being a passenger in this thing. He whips around like a maniac, taking corners sharply and changing lanes without warning. He's zinging and zipping around like he's driving a damn go-kart, and by the time we grab coffees and make it to the dress shop, I'm about three seconds away from having a massive panic attack.

"Oh lord!" I cry out when he parallel parks like a pro. I'm pretty sure even after ten tries, I'd still be attempting to fit my tiny car into the spot. Despite his protests for me to wait, I exit the vehicle on shaky legs, needing to get out before I freak out.

"You could have waited, you know," he says once he catches up to me. I don't miss how he tugs his baseball cap down on his head, and I want to tell him it's no use.

He's a six-foot-three giant with the build of a damn Greek statue. Famous athlete or not, he's going to be noticed anywhere he goes.

"And you could have driven a lot less like you were Lewis Hamilton."

"You know who Lewis Hamilton is?"

"Um, have you *seen* him? Of course I know who he is."

Miller scoffs, then places his hand on my lower back and leads me toward the shop. I spend the entire thirty-second walk trying not to pass out from the feel of his fingers grazing my skin because I have no rational reactions when it comes to Miller.

We stop in front of the door, and he peers down at me, those barley colored eyes of his boring down into me. "You ready?"

To shop with Grady Miller? To have him witness the absolute monster I turn into whenever I'm trying on clothes because I get irritated and hot and dislike everything I put on my body?

Not a chance in hell.

As much as I want to, I don't say that.

Instead, I mutter, "As I'll ever be."

CHAPTER 7

We've been in the store for forty minutes, and Scout has tried on no less than ten different dresses.

All of them are wrong.

"No. Next."

"Excuse me?"

I barely glance up from my phone, but it's long enough to see it's still not the right dress. "That's not the one. Next."

She huffs, her hand going to her hip. "You didn't even look."

"I did, and it's a no."

"Miller...come on. I've tried on so many dresses already, and you've said no to every single one. My boobs are sweating, and I'm starving."

"We'll go to lunch after this, I promise. And besides, have there been any dresses that *you* love?"

She chews on her bottom lip, which tells me just what I suspected—no.

Don't get me wrong, she's looked incredible in just

about every single dress minus the one that had feathers —because, well, it had *feathers*—but none of them are *the one*.

"How much longer is this going to take? It's a charity fundraiser, not a red-carpet event."

I sigh, then look over at the shopkeeper, who is watching all of this unfold. "Can you grab the forest green one?"

Her eyes light up, and she nods enthusiastically before turning away to grab it.

"What forest green one? And why are you saying things like *forest green*? You're a guy."

"First of all, that's sexist. Men can know colors. Secondly, I like to, uh, color."

She tilts her head. "You like to color?"

"Yeah." My cheeks begin to warm because fuck, now that I'm saying it out loud, it sounds stupid, and for some reason, I really don't want to look stupid in front of Scout.

"Like…in coloring books?"

"*Adult* coloring books, but yeah." I shrug, shifting around in the chair I've been parked on since we arrived. "It's relaxing. Sometimes it's helpful after stressful stretches of games."

Her lips pull into a smile. "That's cute."

I narrow my eyes. "I feel like you're making fun of me."

"I'm not!" she insists. "I honestly think it's—"

"Cute?"

"Yeah. Cute." Another grin. "It's...you."

I like the way she says that, like it's something she means, like it's a good thing.

"Here's that dress," the shopkeeper says, thrusting it into Scout's arms.

She looks down at it, confused. "Where did this come from?"

I lift a shoulder. "It was on one of the racks you didn't look at."

"Yeah, because I don't want anything strapless. I... don't have the arms for strapless."

I want to walk up to her, grab her by the shoulders, and shake her because she's clearly out of it if she thinks there's a single thing wrong with any part of her body.

"Try the dress on, Scout."

She eyes the fabric draped over her arms, mulling it over.

I *know* she's going to love the dress if she just gives it a try. I know she's going to love it because I love it, and I want her to see herself from my point of view.

"Please," I add, and she finally looks up at me.

"Fine," she says with a soft sigh, shaking her head like she can't believe she's about to actually do it, then she slips behind the curtain.

The shopkeeper looks over at me, grinning like a fool because I bet she knows what I know—that Scout is about to walk out of that dressing room looking like a million bucks.

"I'm going to go check on the front, but I'll be right back," the woman says to me.

I nod my thanks, she disappears, and I wait.

Then wait some more.

And more.

After what feels like twenty minutes, I can't take it any longer. I rise and make my way over to the dressing room.

"Scout?" I call out softly.

She lets out a loud yelp and flings the curtain open. "Jesus, Miller! You scared me!"

She's glaring at me, I'm sure, but I can't be bothered to care right now.

Because this dress? This dress is *the one*.

It's hugging her everywhere it should be—her tits, her waist, and her ass. And the slit up the front? It's so fucking hot. It's just enough to tease but not enough to be inappropriate. I'm already sad I'm going to have to wait so long to see her in it again.

She looks… "Stunning."

"Huh?"

Fuck. Did I say that out loud?

I clear my throat, then drag my eyes back up her body to her face. "You look stunning, Scout."

Her cheeks turn redder than I've ever seen them get. "Stop it."

The words are whispered.

"What?"

"Stop it," she repeats, a little louder this time.

"Why?"

"Because you don't mean it."

"I don't?"

She shakes her head. "No. You're just saying that because I'm doing you a favor by being your date and you feel obligated. Or maybe you still feel bad about not recognizing me. Or—"

Her words are cut off when I begin stalking toward her.

She takes a step back. I take another forward.

Back. Forward.

Back. Forward.

Like I'm a fucking lion, and she's my prey.

I have no clue what's come over me. All I know is I can't stand here and listen to her not believe me.

"Miller..." She says it quietly, and I'm not quite sure if she's asking me to come closer or to step away.

"I want to set a few things straight, Scout."

She swallows thickly.

I lean closer, trying not to get drunk on the sweet scent of baked goods that seems to cling to her skin. "I'm not saying anything because I'm *obligated* to. I'm saying it because I mean it. Also, I will never lie to you, ever. If I say you're stunning, it's because I believe you are. And you are, Scout. You're stunning."

Her breath hitches, and her pupils dilate at my words. She's peering up at me with those damn hazel eyes she won't stop rolling, and we're trapped together inside the small changing room. I have a feeling I could do anything I wanted to her right now, and she'd let me.

Like kiss her. And at this moment, I really want to kiss her.

I don't know where the thought comes from. I also have no fucking clue how I'm supposed to feel about it, especially since we're just supposed to be friends.

I do know I hate the way she's talking about herself, hate that she can't see how gorgeous she looks right now.

"You're stunning, and I wish you could see it."

I spin her around until she's facing the mirror.

I grab her waist to help keep her steady—or at least that's what I tell myself. Really, it's just an excuse to touch her because I really want to fucking touch her.

"See this dress?" I say, dropping my lips to her ear, loving the way she shivers at our proximity. "See the way it hugs every inch of your body?"

She nods.

"See how gorgeous you look? It's like this dress was made for you, Scout. Like they saw your body, and they knew they had the perfect garment for it."

Unable to stop myself, I drag my fingertips along her arm. I trace a path from her wrist all the way up to her collarbone, then back down again. With every stroke, her breaths grow quicker.

I should stop touching her. I know that. But I can't, and I don't want to.

I don't think she wants me to either.

I need to, though. Every second I spend close to

her...every time I feel her skin under my fingertips...my cock grows harder.

"Do you believe me now?"

She nods slowly.

"Say it."

"I believe you."

The words are shaky and unconvincing.

"Again."

She rolls her tongue along her bottom lip, letting her eyes wander over her reflection in the mirror. She takes in the way the deep green dress wraps around her body. The way it pushes her tits up high—so high, in fact, they're almost to the point of spilling out. The way it wraps around her waist, creating a soft bunch of material that leads to a slit that comes dangerously close to showing everyone just what she's wearing underneath. The way it truly does feel like this dress was made for her.

She tips her chin up higher and straightens her back a little more.

Then, she says, "I believe you."

And this time, I believe her.

"Since you picked our shopping destination, does that mean I get to pick lunch?" I ask, looking over at Scout in the passenger seat.

The dress is tucked safely in the back seat, along with a pair of gold heels she wouldn't stop eying.

"I suppose. But no sushi." She shudders. "I can't stomach it."

"That's a travesty." I swap lanes seamlessly, but I don't miss how she clutches the handle as if I'm out here driving like a madman. "Pizza? I know a really good place. Best pizza in town."

"I won't lie, I'm a hard sell on pizza because there's a place where I grew up that has the best pizza ever, but I'll give it a go."

"Best pizza ever, huh?"

"Yep." She says it so confidently. "Have you ever had macaroni pizza?"

"Isn't that just cheese pizza?"

"That's incredibly offensive. It's pizza with macaroni on it."

"That sounds…"

"Like heaven?" She sighs. "I know. There's also a chicken tender pizza, which is *so* good. And there's a stuffed-crust one with bacon and jalapeños. Don't even get me started on their dessert pizzas."

She moans. Like full-on moans.

I'm not ashamed to admit I find it hot. Hell, I've been sporting a half-chub since we walked out of that dressing room. It's been distracting, to say the least.

I pull the car into the pizzeria and reverse into a spot, shifting the car into park.

She snorts out a laugh. "Of course you're one of those guys."

I don't even get to ask her what she means before she's out of the car. I have a feeling she's not a big fan of my driving.

When we make it into the restaurant, which is a "seat yourself" type thing, I steer Scout toward a table in the back. I know if I happen to get recognized, I'm less likely to be bothered back here.

We grab the menus from the table and begin perusing them. It's nice sitting here with her, not having the need to fill the silence that's stretching between us. It feels comfortable.

"Mr. Miller!"

I pop my head up at the name being called loudly from across the room. The owner of the pizzeria has his arms outstretched and a giant smile across his face as he makes his way toward our table.

"John!" I call back to him, just as excited to see him as he is to see me. I stand and fold my arms around him in a hug. He's a small guy, and I always laugh when I think of how ridiculous we must look hugging.

"It's good to see you, kid," he says, patting my back a few times before letting me go. "You've spent too much time away. We need to fix that." He points at me, narrowing his eyes.

"The season is starting soon, so I'll be back in regularly. I promise."

Hockey players are known to be quite superstitious,

and most of them have their own rituals before games, like taping their sticks a certain way or listening to certain playlists. Hell, even Wayne Gretzky himself had his famous Diet Coke ritual.

Mine includes pizza.

I know, I know. It sounds insane, but it works for me. I carbo-load on pizza, nap, then play.

So, before every home game, I come here to Johnny Boy's Pizza & Pasta.

"Good." He pats my shoulder, then his eyes drift toward Scout, who is still seated, staring up at us with a smile. "Ah! I see you brought a friend today."

I wave toward Scout. "John, meet Scout. She's the genius behind Scout's Sweets over on Eighth."

John's eyes light up. "Those donuts are amazing."

"Thank you." Her cheeks redden. "It's great to meet you, John. I'm excited to try your pizza. Miller won't stop gushing about it."

"This kid, huh? He's great for business." John elbows me. "What're you having to drink? I'll grab 'em for ya."

"I'll take a root beer," Scout says.

"You already know what I want."

He waves a hand my way. "Yeah, yeah. You want the cherry shit. I got ya."

I settle back at the table as he walks away. Scout's grinning at me over the menu.

"What?" I ask her.

She shakes her head. "Nothing. You're just...a little different than I expected, is all."

"Good different?"

She nods. "Yes."

We leave it at that, mostly because I have no clue how to decipher the look in her eye as she says this. It's somewhere between curiosity, disbelief, and happiness. I'm not sure what any of it means.

John drops our drinks off at the table, and we place an order for a large cheeseburger pizza—sans onions, per Scout's request. Blasphemous if you ask me, but whatever.

"So, Scout...is that a nickname?" I ask, ripping the paper off my straw and dunking it into my "cherry shit" or just Cheerwine as I like to call it.

"Nope. It's just Scout. A lot of people think it's a nickname, though. Or at least they want it to be because they don't like it." She shrugs. "But Pops was a big literature fan, and I guess it's some character or something."

"You never read the book you were named after?"

"Nah. Not really my thing."

"What is your thing?" I ask. "I mean, you are a reader, right? I assume that's why you always have the little library out in front of the truck, yeah?"

"I'm definitely a reader. I, uh, prefer romance novels." She tucks a loose strand of hair behind her ear, then rubs her lobe between two fingers. She's fidgeting. "I write them too."

I'm intrigued. "Why do you sound so nervous telling me that?"

"Most people don't take too well to that admission. They either judge and turn their noses up, or they think I'm some sex-crazed maniac."

"And are you? Some sex-crazed maniac?"

She laughs loudly. "Ha! As someone who hasn't had sex in…" She trails off, biting her bottom lip and then shaking her head. "No."

Wait a minute. Is Scout…

"I mean, I'm not a virgin or anything," she says. *Oh. Well, never mind.* "That would be a good storyline, though, wouldn't it? A virgin romance novelist. I'm sure it's already been done. But, yeah, no. Not sex-crazed, not a virgin. Just an author—or wannabe author."

"You haven't published any books?"

Her shoulders deflate. "I haven't even *finished* a book."

"Why not?"

"Well…" She sighs. "I have the truck. It eats up a lot of my time—which is great. I'm super thankful for that, but…I also want to write."

"Then write."

She twists her lips. "It's a little more complicated than that."

"Why?"

"I… I'm blocked."

"Then get unblocked."

"If only it were that easy," she mumbles. "I haven't touched my book in three years."

"I'm no expert, but I feel like three years is a long time not to write for someone who wants to be a writer."

She nods. "It is. But the last time I wrote anything…" She lets out a long breath and sinks lower into the booth. "It was before my dad passed."

My heart sinks, not because I know what it's like to lose a parent, but because of the way her face darkens, the way everything about her just seems to deflate as she says the words. It's clear it was hard on her.

It also makes me feel like an ass because when she said she made a donut for her dads, I just assumed they were both still alive.

"Shit, Scout. That sucks."

"It's okay. I mean, I have another one, but—"

I cough out a surprised laugh, nearly choking on my Cheerwine. "Holy fuck."

"Sorry." She winces. "Dead gay dad joke…too much?"

"No." I shake my head, trying to get my breath back under control. "Just was not expecting that."

"Sometimes I default to dark humor when I get uncomfortable about it." She fidgets with her straw. "I get uncomfortable about it a lot, probably because I don't talk about it often. Or at least that's what my therapist Stevie says."

"Your therapist's name is Stevie?"

"My therapist *is* Stevie."

"I didn't know she was a therapist."

Scout laughs. "She's not. She's just an older sister, and they love to pretend they're therapists like they have everything in life figured out or something, never mind they're just trying to navigate their own issues. I'm sure you understand, though."

"While I do have an older sister, she wasn't around too much when I was younger. There's a nine-year age difference and she split the second she turned eighteen, so I felt like an only child for a long time."

"Really?"

"Yep."

"How was that?" I grimace, and she doesn't miss it. "Uh-oh. That bad?"

"It was…" I lift a shoulder. "Something. On the one hand, I had all of my parents' attention. On the other… well, I had all of my parents' attention. Which, if you're Grady Miller, a kid who seems to be bound for many years of great hockey, can be very exhausting."

The corners of her mouth tug down in a frown. "I'm sorry, Miller. That sounds hard."

It fucking sucked, but I don't tell her that. It doesn't seem right when she's telling me about her dead father.

"Do you and your sister at least get along?"

"We do now. After she moved out, it was like she became a completely different person. She lives out in Seattle with my nephew. I don't get to see them as often as I'd like, but with the new team out there, it's at least a couple of times a year. What about your dad? How was he?"

"He was amazing." A wistful smile plays on her lips. "We had a lot in common. He was a huge book nerd, and because of that, *I* became one too. We could talk about books for hours and never get tired of it, no matter how much it drove Stevie and Dad nuts. He's the reason I want to be a writer."

It's clear by the way she talks about him that he meant a great deal to her, and not just because he was her dad. It sounds like he was her best friend too. I can't imagine losing both in one swoop like that.

"And the reason you can't write?"

She nods. "Afraid so. I promised him I'd finish my book, but…"

"But?"

"It's not pleasant," she warns.

I gesture for her to go on, far too curious about what she's going to say.

She sighs, sitting forward, resting her chin on her hand. "I had a very serious boyfriend when Pops died. We were together for a few years, had an apartment, and I thought he was going to be the one. I loved him, you know?"

"Why do I get the feeling he's about to do some really douchey shit?"

"Oh, because he is." She lets out a dry, humorless laugh. "I guess dating someone who just lost their parent was too hard for him. So, he broke up with me in the worst way: he banged someone else…at my father's funeral."

I swear I see red.

I've never understood that statement before right this moment, but I get it now. It's like a blinding rage. The urge to pummel someone, the absolute carnal need for violence…

I feel that.

Who does that shit? Who treats someone like that, let alone someone who just lost their parent? What kind of person stoops that low?

"What's his name?"

Her brows lift. "Excuse me?"

"His name."

"Miller…"

"What." It's not a question, mostly because I can't fathom why she'd expect anything else right now.

She slides her hand across the table, covering mine with it. The storm brewing inside of me starts to simmer at her touch, and it's only then that I realize my hands are balled into fists.

"Hey," she says softly, drawing my attention away from where she's touching me. "While I appreciate your anger, it's okay. I'm okay."

"It's not okay, Scout."

She gives me a half-smile. "You're right. It's not. But it was a long time ago, and I'm working to move past it. Stevie says I'm kind of stuck in the past sometimes, and I think she may be right. It's time for me to move on, you know?"

I'm not sure if she's saying this to me or to herself, but I nod anyway.

"Okay. But…please tell me you at least decked the guy when you found out."

She grins. "Oh yeah—broke his nose. I kind of understand why you guys like fighting in hockey. It's exhilarating."

"Hot pizza!" John says, appearing at the end of the table.

We break apart, and I instantly miss her hand on mine, but I don't say that.

Instead, I grin at the owner and thank him for the meal.

"Anytime. Enjoy."

Scout slides a piece onto her plate, then hands me the spatula so I can dig in.

"Ready to have your mind blown?" I ask.

She looks at the pie skeptically. "We'll see."

She lifts the slice, gives it a sniff. Takes a small, tentative bite. Chews, swallows, then takes another.

It's the second bite that gets her to crack, and she lets out a soft moan.

"Okay, fine. This is really good. It's not Slice good, but it'll do as a runner-up."

"Told ya." I dig into my food, and we eat in silence for several minutes.

Just as she finishes her first slice, she says, "Hey, Miller?"

I peek up from my food to find her staring at me with serious eyes. "Yeah?"

"Thanks."

"What for?"

"For wanting to stand up for me. It…it means a lot."

"Of course," I say, swallowing down the emotion building in my throat. "That's what friends are for, right?"

Her lips twitch. "Right."

"For what it's worth, I think you should finish your book."

"You haven't even read it—you don't know if it's good or not."

"Nah, doesn't matter. I believe in you all the same."

Her mouth opens like she's surprised to hear the words, but like she needed to hear them too. Finally, after several seconds of silence, she says, "Okay. I'll finish it."

My chest swells with excitement, and we don't talk for the rest of the meal.

CHAPTER 8

SCOUT

I lied to Miller.

I'm never going to finish this book.

I'll never finish it because I've been sitting at this damn desk for an hour and have exactly seven words typed up.

Title Here: A Novel by Scout Thomas

I don't even have a damn title!

I have ideas. Oh, man, do I have ideas. I have a literal notebook that just says *Ideas*, for crying out loud. I've sifted through it no less than ten times, but none of them feel right.

This whole process is stressing me out so much I'd rather be at my donut truck stressing about how I'm going to find another baker.

I've had a few interviews over the last week since my shopping trip with Miller, but just like all the ideas in that notebook, none feel right. I have one more set up for tomorrow before the fundraiser, and if it doesn't work out, I've decided I'm just going to run the truck by myself for the foreseeable future because I am not cut out for the hiring part of this job. Nobody ever said running your own business would be this exhausting, but dang am I tired.

Which is probably why my brain isn't currently functioning. It definitely doesn't have anything to do with the fact that I'm going on a date with a pro hockey player tomorrow, and I'm certainly not so nervous I wasn't even able to finish my glass of wine last night.

He's been stopping by the truck almost every day. He's only missed coming by once due to a press thing, and I'll admit it felt weird not to have him there. I have no idea how I'm going to cope with him actually being gone for the season. Guess I'll find out on Monday when they leave for their first preseason trip.

It's a little ridiculous how used to him I've become. He was always a frequent flyer at the truck before, but now it's more than that. Sometimes I have to actually kick him out and make him go away because he's being obnoxious, which seems to be par for the course with him.

I won't lie…it's been nice having him around, especially since I'm solo-ing it at the moment. It makes time go by faster and keeps me distracted in a good way.

Plus, he's not bad to look at.

Yeah, it's safe to say my little crush on him is still intact. Hell, it may even be worse after the incident in the dressing room.

I have no idea what came over him, no idea why he

cornered me, why he touched me and made me feel like we were the only two people on the planet.

But he did all of those things and then some.

I was so uncertain about how I looked in the dress, afraid it was showing off too many of my stomach rolls, clinging a little too tightly to the dimples on my ass, showing entirely too much boob. But when Miller called me stunning and made me really look at myself, I didn't see any of those things anymore.

All I saw was the way he was looking at me.

And I liked it.

Maybe I could conjure that feeling again—as if I haven't several times this week—and channel it into my writing.

I position my fingers at the keyboard and begin to type.

"Knock, knock!" Stevie calls out, tapping her knuckles against my door, interrupting me. She pushes it open, popping her head around the corner. "Dinner's ready."

"Macaroni and cheese?"

"Of course—it's Thursday."

Every Thursday for the last year, Macie makes mac and cheese. I swear it's how I'm able to tell what day it is half the time.

Sometimes she'll add something to it like ground beef or tuna. Sometimes it's hot dogs, and once she did jalapeños, but it's always mac and cheese of some sort. I love that she has the cooking bug, but sometimes I wish she'd branch out a little more. There's only so much cheese and noodles a person can eat.

Stevie's eyes bounce to my open laptop. They widen when she reads the screen.

I slam the computer shut and rise from the world's most uncomfortable chair, which I deeply regret purchasing. Maybe that's my issue, why I'm unable to write.

I laugh to myself because I know it's not.

"Whatcha working on these days?" Stevie asks not so casually.

"Nothing." Technically it's not a lie because that's what I typed—nothing.

But we both know me just sitting at the computer staring at a blank document *was* something. It's been over a year since I've done even that.

I want to write. I truly do, but my fingers don't seem to work every time I sit down. Stevie's convinced it's because I don't have a life outside the donut truck, and she may be right. I think writing was a massive part of my connection with my father, and my grief blocks me.

Honestly, I'm sure it's a perfect storm of both.

"Whatever you say," she says as I practically shove her out of the door.

We reach the small dining room table just as Macie sets the last bowl down. Before sitting, I grab a bottle of root beer from the fridge, a Diet Coke for Stevie, and a juice box for my niece.

"I added bacon tonight, Aunt Scout!" Macie says from my right as she grabs forks from the drawer.

Okay, fine, the bacon does make me a little more excited for dinner.

"I bet it's going to be amazing," I tell her.

"I've almost perfected the recipe too." She passes the silverware to her mother and me.

"You've been working on this for a year. Isn't the recipe perfect?"

"Not yet," she insists, sitting down in her chair, tugging it closer to the table with a loud scrape. "But close."

We dive into the food, and it's just as good as all her other concoctions.

"So," Stevie starts, "are you nervous about tomorrow?"

"What's tomorrow?" Macie asks.

"I'm going to a fundraiser the Comets are hosting."

Her eyes widen at this information, and she sits up higher in her chair. "You'll be there with the whole team?"

I nod. "Yep."

"And she's going as Grady Miller's date."

"A date?!" Macie squeaks out, clapping her hands together.

"As *friends*," I clarify, sending a pointed glare Stevie's way. She doesn't break under the weight of it. "It's just as friends."

"You're friends with him?" Macie asks.

"Umm…yes. I guess I am." At this point, I think I might be telling the truth. Sure, I've told Miller we're friends, but not until after our shopping trip and lunch date, when I spilled all of my secrets to him, did I really feel like that might be true.

"Like boyfriend-and-girlfriend kind of friends?"

"No." I shake my head. "Just *friends* friends."

She twists her lips, her face scrunching up like she just ate something sour and doesn't like it. "Hmm. Okay."

Stevie points her fork toward her daughter. "For the record, I'm with her."

"I'm shocked," I deadpan.

I love my sister, but she's driving me nuts about this whole fundraiser thing. She's been dropping hints all week about how she thinks Miller and I would make a cute couple. I keep telling her it's never going to happen, but she doesn't believe me.

"Liar." Stevie sticks her tongue out when Macie isn't looking.

"Can you get me an autographed puck tomorrow?"

"I'm sure I can swing it," I say to my niece, unsurprised by her request. She asked for one when I went to Smith's party too. Luckily, Wright was kind enough to send one home with me for her. "Do you want Miller's signature?"

She scrunches her nose. "No. And not one from the jackass from the truck either."

"Macie!" her mother cries out in protest.

"You said she could say jackass," I point out.

Stevie hangs her head, her shoulders shaking with laughter. "I did say she could say jackass."

"All right, so no autograph from Greer either. Maybe Smith?"

Macie guffaws. "That old man? Nope. I want Beast's. He's dreamy." She bounces her brows up and down. I have no clue if she even knows what dreamy means or if she just heard her mother lusting after Chris Hemsworth again.

"All right. Beast's it is."

"And maybe Coach Heller too?" She folds her hands together, sticking her bottom lip out in a plea. "You'd be my favorite aunt."

"I'm your only aunt."

"Please?"

I sigh, but there's no real annoyance behind it. "Fine. I'll see what I can do."

"Yes!" She fist-pumps the air. "Also, it's your turn to do dishes tonight."

"I'm going to get all these autographs for you, and you're still making me do dishes? I thought I was your favorite aunt."

"You are, but I also hate doing dishes, so…" She shovels the last of her mac and cheese in her mouth, swallows, then hops off her chair. She presses a kiss to my cheek before yelling "Bye!" and running off.

I look at Stevie, who is just shaking her head at her daughter's antics.

"That's your kid," I say.

"I know. Don't you love her?"

"So much." I really truly do. "I hope the guys are cool about the autographed pucks."

"I'm sure they will be. They all always seem nice when they stop by the truck." She takes a bite of her dinner. "Speaking of…now that the little ears are gone, how are you *really* feeling about tomorrow?"

"Like I'm going to vomit."

"Because you're still crushing on Miller, and you're worried seeing him all dressed up in his tux is going to send your lady bits into overdrive, and you'll have to ravage him in the coat closet?"

A laugh bubbles out of me. "I thought I was the storyteller here."

She lifts a shoulder. "What? I have an overactive imagination sometimes, especially when I haven't been laid in ages." She mutters the last part.

She doesn't have to tell me twice. What I didn't finish telling Miller the other day is that I'm not a virgin, but I may as well be. I haven't had sex in three years. Haven't dated in that long either. It feels like a lifetime ago in so many ways.

"I am nervous," I tell her honestly.

She perks up at this. "You are?"

I nod. "Yeah. I… Well, I haven't been out with anyone since Aaron." I wince when I say my ex's name. "While this isn't a date"—I give her a pointed look—"in some ways, it feels like it is. Probably just because the event is fancy, I'm sure."

"Right. Nothing to do with the fact that you're still crushing on Miller."

"Shut up," I tell her. "But yes. He's so…"

"Miller?"

I nod. "Is it weird to describe him that way? By his name?"

"No, not with a guy like him. He's his own brand of…well, him. It's kind of hard not to find him attractive and obnoxious all in one breath. I think you two are going to have a great time tomorrow."

"I hope so." I groan, running my hand through my messy hair. "I can't believe I'm going to be in a room full of hockey players tomorrow. I hope I don't do or say something embarrassing."

"Trust me, I think Miller will embarrass himself enough for the both of you."

I laugh. "True."

"Besides, the wives will be there, right? You can always mingle with them, make some new friends. Live a little, have fun—you deserve it."

For the first time in a long time, I think Stevie's right.

I do deserve it.

This is a lot more than I was expecting it to be.

A camera flashes in my face, which already hurts from smiling so much, and I grip Miller's arm tighter because I'm now too blind to see much of anything.

"Are you okay?" he asks out of the side of his mouth, somehow still smiling at the camera.

I simply squeeze his arm in response because I'm honestly not sure if I am okay. I feel like a fraud and like I look like a million bucks all at once. It's hard to recognize who I am under all this makeup and glam, but it also feels good to try something different.

There's at least another minute of posing and smiling —which doesn't really sound like a long time, but when you have several cameras in your face, it feels like an eternity—before we're finally free and walking through the doors of the event.

"That was intense," I say to Miller once we're inside the massive entrance to the expansive venue.

"I thought the same when I first started playing hockey, but now I'm just kind of used to being bombarded by cameras and microphones. I'm sorry—I should have warned you better. If you had at least allowed me to pick you up, maybe I could have." He lifts his brows disapprovingly.

Miller insisted several times that he wanted to pick me up for the event, but I just couldn't do it. I've already been a nervous wreck all week, and there was no way I'd be able to sit through an entire car ride next to him and not throw up all over the gorgeous gold heels he spent entirely too much money on.

Instead, he sent a limo to my apartment. I felt like such a fool walking from the tiny two-bedroom box to the fancy car.

I shrug. "It was out of the way."

It's a damn lie, and we both know it.

"Are you nervous?" he asks.

This time, I don't lie to him. "I am."

"Don't be. Once we get into the main room, it'll be just like normal."

"Easy for you to say—you're not one who isn't used to dressing up and pretending to be someone you're not. It's a little hard to relax when I look like this." I swoop my hand over my dress, trying to keep up with his long strides.

Without warning, Miller tugs me out of the main entryway and into a smaller hall. There's nobody else over here but us, and I'm keenly aware of that when he crowds me against a wall.

"Miller, what are—"

"Have I told you yet how stunning you look in that dress?"

Heat fills my cheeks, and I have to bite down on my lower lip to control the smile that's dying to break free. "Not today."

"Well, that's on me, huh?" He steps closer, and I'm instantly wrapped in the warmth that's radiating off his big body. "You're stunning, Scout."

I meet his whiskey-colored eyes, my breath getting harder and harder to catch the more I peer into them.

"Thank you," I whisper.

"You're welcome." He gives me his trademark smile.

"Now, let's get you a glass of champagne, huh? Calm those nerves."

I'm almost certain drinking around Miller would be a bad idea. I think I'd say things I shouldn't, do things I normally wouldn't.

But tonight…tonight I don't want to be *just Scout*.

I want to have fun. I want to let loose. I want to feel good.

So, I do the exact opposite of what I should.

I say, "Okay."

And when he holds his hand out, I thread my fingers through his and let him pull me into the night.

CHAPTER 9

I'm not sure if it's the three glasses of champagne that have calmed her nerves, but Scout seems like she's fitting right in. I'm sure it helps that she's already familiar with several of my favorite people on the team, most of whom are currently seated around our table.

She's smiling at the conversation Lowell and Rhodes seem to be stuck in, and I can't help but watch her watch them.

She wore her hair down tonight, something she doesn't do very often. I have this weird urge to pull it off her neck and place my lips there instead because seeing her in that dress again is making my head all fuzzy.

Or maybe it's the vodka I'm drinking.

"No, I'm telling you, Rhodes, it's not going to happen."

"Come on. Then we can tell people we both got married in Vegas."

"We're not even engaged!" Lowell cries out.

"Then propose, moron!" Rhodes argues back.

"Uh, hi," Hollis says, poking her head around her boyfriend. "Do I get a say in this?"

"No," both guys say in unison.

"If it's any consolation, I vote Vegas too," I chime in. "Who doesn't want to get married by Elvis?"

"See!" Rhodes points at me. "For once, I agree with the kid."

"I think you should have a wedding in October," Harper, Wright's wife, says to her sister. "Then you could use pretty pumpkins as décor."

"Again, we're not even engaged. We haven't even talked about marriage." The captain sounds like he's had this exact conversation a thousand times already.

"What? My sister-in-law is good enough for you to impregnate but not marry?" Wright challenges Lowell with a lifted brow.

"Yeah!" Harper nods. "You knock my sister up, then what? Be her boyfriend forever?"

"No!" He shoves out of his chair. "I'm getting a drink."

He stomps off, and everyone at the table laughs. We all know Lowell and Hollis aren't ready to walk down the aisle, but it doesn't mean we can't tease them about it.

"You guys are so mean getting him all wound up," Hollis declares in defense of her boyfriend.

"Yeah, but he plays better when he's mad, and we could really use a win on Monday to kick off the preseason."

She shakes her head, but I'm sure she knows Rhodes is right on the money.

"I'm not looking forward to being the only one on diaper duty," Hollis remarks, talking about her adorable new baby.

"We'll help you, you know that," Harper says, nodding toward Ryan.

"I'll help too," Scout says quietly from beside me. "I mean, if you need it, of course." She dips down in her seat when everyone stares at her. "I have some experience with kids. I helped raise my niece."

"Did you really?" I ask, surprised.

"Yeah." She nods. "Macie's father is…well, he's not in the picture." I can see a cloud of darkness fall over her face. I'm sure there's a story there regarding Macie's dad, but I know now isn't the place to ask for details, not that I'm owed any. "It's just been me, Stevie, and Macie since the day she was brought home from the hospital."

"Gah! Babies are so cute when they're all tiny and squishy," Ryan says fondly. "You just want to boop their little noses."

"Agreed."

"You like kids?" Now it's Scout's turn to be surprised.

I'm one of those weird guys who wants a big family and loves children. I know what an empty home feels like. I don't want that for my future.

I'm about to answer when Harper cuts in.

"They look like aliens. Someone send Sigourney

Weaver to kick some ass, because *ew*." She wrinkles her nose.

Greer points at her. "I'm with this one. Babies and kids are gross."

"Macie thinks you're gross," Scout says to him, a tipsy laugh bubbling out of her. "She calls you the jackass."

Greer's face turns sour, but everyone else laughs.

"Smart kid," Smith remarks.

"She calls you the old man."

"Hey, that's what we call him too," Wright says, earning himself a hard glare from said old man.

"I might be old, but I can still whoop your ass."

"Please. Like I'm scared of you." Wright rolls his eyes just as Smith reaches out and whacks him across the back of his head. For once, I'm not the guy getting hit, and it feels nice not to be picked on.

"Hey! Be nice, or I'll tell Coach," Wright threatens.

"Real mature, honey." Harper pats her husband's cheek.

"I'm mature," he mutters, which doesn't sound mature at all. "Whatever. I'm getting a drink." He rises from his chair.

"Do they have beer at this thing? I can't take any more of this champagne," Rhodes gripes, following behind Wright.

Their wives exchange glances and then go after them.

"So, when did this thing happen between you two?"

asks Emilia, the team's social media director and Smith's girlfriend.

Scout gestures from herself to me. "Us?" Emilia nods, and my date barks out a laugh. "No. We're not... No."

It's not her words that sting, because they're not wrong; it's her laugh—almost like she couldn't fathom dating me, and I'm not sure how I feel about that.

Do I *want* her to want to date me? Or am I just spending so much time with her lately that she's in my head?

"That's right," I say. "We're not together."

"No?" Greer asks from across the table, rolling the bottom of his cup around in circles over the table. "Hm."

I scowl, not liking the sound that just came out of him.

"In that case," he says loudly, rising to his feet. He extends his hand across the table...right to Scout. "May I have this dance?"

"You dance?" She stares at his outstretched hand.

"I took ballroom lessons for my mother's third wedding."

She glances at his hand again, then at him, and back at his hand. Finally, she shrugs. "Why not? Just nobody tell my niece I danced with the jackass."

Greer smirks at her. "It'll be our little secret."

I hate his smirk, and I hate the way Scout smirks back.

I really hate that they have a secret.

Greer pulls Scout out onto the dance floor and tugs her so close her body is snug against his. I know for a fact it's not ballroom etiquette because *I* took ballroom lessons too.

He nuzzles her neck, whispering something into her ear while his fingertips play along the cutout in the back of her dress. Scout throws her head back, laughing at something Greer says.

They look good together. Scout looks happy.

I *should* be happy she's having a good time, should be glad tonight isn't a complete disaster for her.

But I'm not happy because seeing Scout in Greer's arms is making my blood boil. I hate it more than I've ever hated anything in my life.

And I hate that I'm not sure what the hell that's supposed to mean.

"Dude, Miller…" Smith says, and I feel his hand clamp over my own.

I look down and see that my knuckles are turning white against the glass of vodka I've been sipping for the last two hours.

"Are you *sure* there's nothing going on between you two?" Emilia asks.

I hesitate only a moment before nodding my head. "Yes, I'm sure."

"But…"

I swallow, not answering because, from the knowing smile on her face, I'm not so sure I need to.

There isn't anything going on with us.

But I…I think I want there to be.

"Want my advice, kid? Talk to her. Tell her how you feel," Smith says, reading my mind. He looks over at his girlfriend. "It's something I wish I had done a hell of a lot sooner."

I'm out of my seat before I can realize what I'm doing.

I'm crossing the dance floor.

I'm shoving Greer out of the way, and I'm taking his spot.

Distantly, I hear him laugh, but I don't pay him any attention.

All I can focus on is Scout, who is staring up at me with wide eyes as I pull her against me—breaking all ballroom rules myself. She lets out a tiny squeak but doesn't protest the interruption.

I like that she doesn't.

We glide across the floor, not missing a single step, moving in perfect sync with one another.

"This is unexpected," she murmurs quietly.

"I took lessons, too."

She tries to hide her smile, but I see it anyway.

I know how ridiculous I sound, how petty, how childish. But dammit, I don't want Greer to dance with Scout. I don't want him to flirt with her. I don't want him to know what she feels like in his arms because *I* want all those things.

I want Scout.

I…

"Date me."

She rears her head back, completely caught off guard by my words.

The feeling is mutual because I can't believe I just said them.

"What?"

"Date me," I repeat. "I mean…" I clear my throat. "Would you like to go on a date? With me, I mean."

We've stopped moving. I'm not sure when that happened, but we have. Now we're just standing here staring at one another.

And it's fucking unbearable. With every second that ticks by, I feel more and more like a total moron.

Date me? Really? Fuck, it's no wonder I'm still a virgin with dating skills like this.

I should take it back, should tell her to forget it…but I don't want to do either of those things.

I have to say *something*, though, because this is doing nothing short of killing me.

"Scout, I—"

"Okay," she says, and the words die on my tongue.

Now it's me who leans back, surprised. "O…kay?" I draw the word out, making sure she said what I think she did.

She nods. "Yes. I'll go on a date with you."

"I…" I swallow down the excitement. "Okay. We're going on a date."

"Yep."

"It's going to be a good date," I tell her, pulling her back in.

"Okay."

We begin slowly moving to the music. "The best first date you've ever been on."

"That so?"

"Yep. It's going to—"

"Miller?" she interrupts.

"Hm?"

"Don't make me regret this already."

I laugh. "Yes, ma'am."

I firmly believe the only reason Scout is allowing me to drive her home is that she's still a little tipsy from the champagne.

Well, that and I only booked the limo service for one way, so it was either me or an Uber.

She chose me.

"This is my place." She points up at the apartment building in front of us.

I can see under the yellow streetlights that it's a little run down, but it's not as if I was expecting to drop her off at a mansion or anything.

"It's not much," she says like she knows what I'm thinking. "But it's home." She fidgets with the small wristlet purse she brought. "I, uh, live with Stevie."

"You live with your sister?" She winces. "Are you

embarrassed by that? Because you don't have to be. The first year I was with the Comets, I lived with my coach. Now *that's* embarrassing. Talk about awkward when you have to masturbate." *Oh fuck.* "I mean, not that I masturbate. I—"

She throws her head back and laughs, and it reminds me of earlier when Greer made her do the same thing.

"What did Greer say to make you laugh earlier?"

She looks surprised by the sudden change of subject. "Huh?"

I don't know why I care. I shouldn't care, but I do.

"Earlier, when you were dancing with Greer, you laughed like that. What did he say to make you laugh so hard?"

The streetlights are just bright enough that I can still see the red that colors her cheeks.

"He, um, he told me to do that."

My brows squish together. "Huh?"

"He told me to laugh like he just told me something funny because he wanted to test something."

"He wanted to…" *Holy shit.* I shake my head. "That asshole. He was testing me, wasn't he?"

She nods. "Afraid so."

"And it worked."

"It did, but…" She lets out a heavy breath, and I brace myself for her to tell me she's taking back agreeing to a date, it's a mistake, and she doesn't want to ruin our —reluctant on her part—friendship or something. "I'vehadacrushonyouforawhile."

It comes out in one big, long word, and I'm certain she didn't just say what I think she did.

"What?"

She groans, cradling her face in her hands, then realizes a few moments too late that she's wearing makeup and that's probably not a good idea. She sinks down into her seat and takes another fortifying breath.

"I've had a crush on you for a while. So, I wasn't really mad about it."

My brows shoot up. "You've been crushing on me?"

The red on her cheeks deepens as she nods. "Yes."

"For how long?"

"Since you've been coming to the truck."

Oh fuck. That makes me feel kind of awful.

I've seen Scout at the truck so many times over the years, but I never really *saw* her until recently, and I can't believe what I've been missing out on.

"I never knew," I say quietly.

"I know." She tucks her lips together like she's hurt by this, but also maybe not surprised. "It's okay."

"It's not. The guys on the team are right—I am a fucking idiot."

Her brows furrow. "Stop saying that. You're not an idiot. You're not stupid. You're just...well, you're Miller."

"Is that a bad thing?"

She shakes her head. "Not at all. I happen to like Miller."

"As a *friend*?"

"Or more." She blushes again, then clears her throat. "Anyway, this is me."

I laugh. "Yeah, you said that." I point at her. "Wait here."

She giggles but remains in the car while I hop out. I jog over to her side and pull her door open, bending at the waist in a dramatic fashion.

She laughs again, and I swear I love the sound of it more every time I hear it.

She slips her hand into mine, allowing me to help her from the vehicle.

"Come on. I'll walk you up."

"You don't—oh, okay," she says when she sees the look I'm sending her, daring her to keep challenging me.

Unsure of where to go exactly, I let her lead the way, but I keep my hand on her lower back the entire way because I can't seem to stop touching her.

My fingers rest against exposed skin. It's warm and soft, and I want to touch more of her.

But I'm getting way ahead of myself.

We stop in front of a door that has a Carolina Comets-themed wreath on it, and I can't help but laugh.

"I'm sure it's just because Macie is a big fan, but I'm going to pretend it was you who picked that out so you could support your best friend."

"Best friend, huh?" Her lips pull into a half-smile. "Wow, we're moving fast."

"It's because you can't get enough of me, always wanting me to be around."

"Whatever you need to tell yourself to help you sleep at night."

"Oh, I don't need to tell myself anything. I sleep just fine knowing how obsessed with me you are, Miss Crushing on Me for Months over here."

"You know, the more you talk, the more I'm really starting to doubt my sanity."

"Nah. You like me."

She rolls her eyes. "Despite your inability to get over yourself, I had a really nice time tonight."

"Yeah?" She nods. "Good. I did too. Especially the part where you agreed to a date with me."

She groans. "Ugh. I did, huh?"

"Yep, and I'm holding you to it—though it may not be until I get back from these two preseason games…"

"That's fine. I'm sure I'm going to need time to prepare myself for it."

"I promise to make it not suck."

"Mm, we'll see about that." She grabs hold of the door handle. "Thanks again."

"Anytime."

She doesn't move. Neither do I.

We stand there in silence for several seconds, letting the cool, September night air settle between us.

"I…um…good night," she says.

"Good night."

She laughs, dropping her eyes to where our fingers are still laced. "I kind of need my hand back, Miller."

"Right. But here's the thing—I kind of don't want to let go."

"Kind of?"

"More than kind of. I definitely don't want to let go."

I don't want to let go because I'm scared if I do, she's going to come to her senses and tell me the date is off, and I really don't want that.

I like Scout. I like her a lot.

"But…" I draw the word out. "I suppose I'll allow it."

"Thank you," she says, but it seems like she doesn't want to let me go either because I swear this is the slowest anyone has ever stopped touching someone else.

When we finally let go, it feels weird, like I'm missing something vital. I've never felt that before.

"Good night."

"You said that already."

"Well, this time I mean it." She spins around, digging into her purse for her key like she's trying to prove a point.

I can't help but laugh.

She glares over her shoulder at me.

I laugh harder.

"Stop it, Miller. I'll take our date back."

I gasp dramatically. "You wouldn't dare."

"Try me." She finally retrieves her keys and inserts one into the lock.

"Hey, Scout?"

She sighs loudly, turning my way. "Yes?"

I take a step closer, closing the short distance between

us. She gasps softly at my sudden movements but doesn't shift back.

I swallow the knot lodged in my throat as she stares up at me, waiting.

"I'm sorry I didn't see you before, but I see you now."

Her mouth floats open. Then closes.

Opens again.

Then, I swear she mutters, "Oh, what the hell?"

And her mouth crashes to mine.

I slide my hands over her waist, tugging her closer as she grabs my lapels and does the same. Her back hits the door with a loud thud that will likely wake a sleeping Stevie, but I don't care.

I don't care because I'm kissing her. I'm kissing her, and all I can think is *She tastes as sweet as she smells.*

It's stupid and absurd, but it's exactly what I imagined her lips would taste like.

And I need more.

I run my tongue along her bottom lip. She lets me in, letting out a soft moan when our tongues slide together.

I've kissed many women before, but not even one of those kisses has ever come close to comparing to this. It's soft and unhurried, like we're both afraid to move too fast because then we know it will be over.

I have no idea how long we kiss, how long our bodies are pressed together in the dimly lit hallway, how long we stand there holding on to one another when our mouths finally drift apart. We're a mess of heavy breaths, and I can feel her shiver beneath my fingertips.

I should go. I know I should. I just can't bring myself to move my feet.

I'm not sure how much longer I stand there, but it's long enough to hear her teeth chattering, and I know then that I've overstayed my welcome.

So, with reluctance, I place one last kiss on her forehead and whisper, "Good night, Scout."

"Good night…Grady."

I swear, I've never loved my name more.

CHAPTER 10

MILLER & SCOUT

Miller: Did you know it's a really bad idea to eat four hot dogs, a hamburger, and a milkshake before skating?

Miller: I didn't do that. Some rookie on the other team did and barfed all over the ice. Totally disgusting.

Scout: Who is this?

Miller: What do you mean?

Miller: It's Miller.

Scout: Who?

. . .

Miller: M-I-L-L-E-R

Miller: As in...IT'S MILLER TIME, BABY!

Scout: You know, I was going to keep this going longer, but you just ruined everything with that horrible pun, and I'm considering blocking you.

Miller: Nah. You wouldn't.

Scout: And why not?

Miller: Because I'm a really good kisser?

Scout: Are you asking me that or telling me?

Miller: Telling.

Miller: Or maybe asking.

.   .   .

Miller: You know, I'm really not sure, mostly because now I'm curious what you thought of our kiss.

Miller: So…what'd you think of our kiss?

Scout: There really is no beating around the bush with you, is there?

Miller: About 98% of the time, no.

Scout: And the other 2%?

Miller: I'm not ready for the other 2% just yet.

Scout: That's fair.

Scout: Did someone get sick during the game?

Miller: Warmups.

. . .

Miller: I kind of felt bad for the guy. I've been the young, dumb rookie before. It's rough sometimes.

Scout: You say that like you're not still young and dumb.

Miller: Hey, I'm 24, thank you very much.

Miller: Still dumb, though.

Scout: You're 24?!

Miller: Yup.

Miller: Wait—how old are you?

Miller: Actually, no. Never mind. I know you're not supposed to ask women that.

Scout: Such a stupid rule.

. . .

Scout: I'm 28.

Miller: Oh, I've snagged an older lady. Nice.

Scout: Snagged?

Scout: OLDER LADY?

Scout: Keep it up. At this rate, you're going to be the one in the grave first, not me.

Miller: I'm assuming you're going to be the death of me?

Scout: Yes.

Scout: Here lies Grady Miller. He died because he talked too much shit.

Miller: That honestly checks out, though.

. . .

Scout: Have you always been this way?

Miller: Yes. My parents didn't love me enough as a child.

Miller: Sadly, that last part isn't a lie. They really didn't.

Miller: Womp, womp.

Scout: Okay, that's just depressing.

Miller: Sorry.

Scout: I'M sorry.

Miller: Eh, don't be. It is what it is.

Scout: That's a very sad way of looking at it.

. . .

Miller: It's practical.

Scout: Since when are you ever practical?

Miller: That's fair.

Miller: I gotta go, but I just wanted you to know I was thinking about you.

Scout: Miller, you literally texted me about someone vomiting, so I'm not sure that's the compliment you think it is.

Miller: If it makes you feel any better, I was thinking about you before the vomit.

Scout: Gee, thanks.

Scout: For what it's worth, I was thinking about you too…and our kiss.

. . .

Scout: A-

Miller: I've always been told I'm an overachiever, so now I guess I have something to work toward.

Scout: ??

Miller: An A+

Scout: I'm stingy with pluses.

Miller: I bet I'm worth making an exception for.

Scout: We'll see about that.

Miller: What about Thursday?

Scout: It's a very disappointing day of the week, mostly because it's not Friday.

. . .

Scout: Though to be fair, I don't really get weekends off, so Fridays kind of suck too.

Scout: I'm sure you know all about that, though.

Miller: I do, but I meant what about Thursday for our date?

Miller: Unless you'd like to choose a less disappointing day of the week.

Scout: Honestly, they all suck in some way. Except for Saturday. Saturdays are wine-in-the-tub nights.

Scout: But Thursday is fine.

Miller: Wine in the tub?

Scout: Yep. I light candles, crank the Taylor Swift, drink the fanciest of wines, and relax.

. . .

Miller: That sounds…nice.

Scout: Even the Taylor Swift?

Miller: Are you kidding me? Especially the Taylor Swift.

Scout: Oh, so you're a fan?

Miller: All I'm saying is there is no way in hell Jake doesn't still have that scarf.

Scout: Right? He totally kept it!

Scout: Good luck at your game tonight.

Miller: Are you watching?

Scout: If being in the same living room as Macie as she screams at the TV for you to shoot counts as watching, then yes.

. . .

Miller: It's preseason! I'm saving all my good shots for when it counts.

Scout: Try telling Coach Macie that.

Miller: She's going to be one tough cookie.

Scout: Going to be? She already is.

Scout: How about some motivation? If you win, I'll let you buy dinner, and if you lose, I'll let you buy dinner.

Miller: So, I'm buying dinner either way?

Scout: Of course you are. It's a date.

Miller: That's not very feminist of you.

Scout: No, it's not. But I'm also not a super-rich hockey player.

. . .

Miller: I wouldn't say super rich. That'd be Lowell.

Scout: You make more a year than I'll ever make in a lifetime.

Miller: Did you Google me?

Scout: Of course I did. I like to know whom I'm dating.

Miller: That's fair.

Miller: I'm going to Google you later, just so we're even.

Scout: That sounds mildly sexual.

Miller: It does, doesn't it?

Scout: Totally.

· · ·

Miller: I gotta go. Coach Smith is yelling at me.

Miller: See you Thursday.

Miller: And, Scout? I'm really looking forward to working on my grade.

CHAPTER 11

I'm beginning to think something might be seriously wrong with me.

That's the only reason I can conceive of for saying yes to so many things involving Miller. First his apology, then accepting his help with my truck, then the fundraiser.

And now? I said yes to a date.

A date! Me and Miller. Alone. Together. Doing date things.

I can't believe it.

Just like I still can't believe I kissed him.

I freaking kissed Miller!

My face heats and my lips get all tingly just thinking about it and the way he pressed me against the door and kissed me somehow harder and softer than anyone ever has before.

It's all that has been consuming my thoughts for the last week while he's been tied up in the preseason. They played two road games, came home and hit the ice hard with practice, then had two more away games. I haven't seen him since the night of the fundraiser, and as much as I hate to admit it, I miss him. Miller being gone is just as strange as I thought it would be. It's like my whole routine is thrown off, which is ridiculous because he's just a customer.

A customer I kissed and am going on a date with, but still. I'm not going to get ahead of myself and think anything of it. I can't let my mind wander there.

"Where do we keep the apple pie spice?"

I look over at the newest employee of Scout's Sweets, Rosie, then point toward the counter she's standing right in front of.

"Second shelf, right there next to the nutmeg." I can't help but think of Miller when I say it, which has a smile curving my lips.

"You got it, boss."

She bends and starts shoving spices around, moving the older containers to the front and putting the new ones in the back.

Rosie started last week, and things have been great so far. There were a few learning curves with the equipment, but she's getting the hang of it fast, and it's truly been a relief to have help. I have a feeling she's going to stick around, which means I'm finally going to have some free time to write, something I've been itching to do every free second I get.

After Miller kissed the hell out of me, I wrote five hundred words. Five hundred! That's more than I've done in years. I mean, when I read them all back, I decided they were trash and deleted them, but it's still progress.

"What has you smiling?" Stevie asks, appearing out of nowhere. She sets her purse on the hook by the back door and then leans against one of the counters.

"She's been doing that all day," Rosie says, ratting me out as she organizes the spices.

"Is it because a certain hockey player is taking you out on a date tonight?" My sister bounces her brows up and down, and I glower at her.

I wasn't planning on telling her about my date with Miller, but I didn't have a choice. After I finally regained my senses after kissing Miller and went inside, I about had a heart attack because Stevie was sitting in the dark living room, waiting up for me.

She heard everything. Every word. Every moan. All of it.

And she couldn't stop grinning. Wouldn't stop asking questions until I finally told her everything.

Sometimes I think she's more excited about the date than I am.

We've been texting off and on while he's not been around and finally settled on going on our date tomorrow. I have no idea where we're going. All he said was to wear a dress and heels, and for some reason that makes me ten times more nervous about it.

"I still can't believe the Comets come here all the time," Rosie says. "I'm a huge hockey fan. I have no idea how I'm going to contain myself—especially if Fitzgerald, that new trade from Vancouver, stops by." She fans herself, then looks sheepish. "Sorry. I get a bit excited about hockey."

Stevie lifts her hands. "No judgments from me. There are a lot of hot guys on the ice, that's for sure."

"And who do you think is hot?" I lift a brow, curious.

"Uno reverse!" she calls out, avoiding the question.

I groan. "Not fair."

"Is too!"

"What's Uno reverse?" Rosie asks.

"It means she's putting the question back on me."

"And Scout here doesn't want that because she'll have to say she thinks Miller is hot, and she doesn't like to admit her little crush." Stevie grins triumphantly, clearly feeling really proud of herself right now.

I scowl at her, but she doesn't care.

"Okay, but Miller *is* hot," Rosie says. "So, no shame in that."

I've never really been a jealous person before. It's not in my nature.

But when Rosie says Miller is hot, I swear a streak of it runs straight through me because I can picture Miller sending her flirty smiles and using cheesy pick-up lines on her, and I hate it.

I hate it so much my teeth grind against each other.

"But Fitzgerald is more my style," Rosie says, and just as quickly as the streak appeared, it's gone. "I assume Miller is the one you're going on a date with?"

"Miller is the one she also shamelessly made out with against our front door last week."

"Stevie!"

"Wow. I didn't know I'd be getting all this juicy gossip this early on." Rosie rubs her hands together. "Tell me more. What was it like? Is he a good kisser? I follow some hockey gossip sites and have seen him with some other women before, but nothing long term."

I frown because as much as I don't like admitting it, I've seen it too.

After I let the evening of the fundraiser settle, I jumped right to the last place I needed to be—Google. I couldn't find any information on his dating history aside from a few photos of him at various fancy-schmancy restaurants around the city with women who looked like they could be on runways. None of them looked particularly serious, but there was one thing I could say for certain about them—all the women were my exact opposite.

Which makes me wonder, of all the women available to him, why did Miller ask *me* out? Why did he kiss *me*?

"There's not much to tell."

"Liar!" Stevie interjects. "You said—and I quote— 'Kissing Miller was better than soaking in the tub with a slice of cake and a glass of wine after a long day.' Said it was 'better than sex with Jacob Karlsson, the guy from college who had the nine-inch cock and could eat pussy like a pro.'"

"Stevie!" I hiss at her, my face flaming red, I'm sure.

"Oh my god." Rosie doubles over in laughter, probably at the pure shock that's etched across my face. "I was not expecting that from you at all."

"Because I didn't say that!"

Okay, fine. I totally did say that.

And I meant it too. Kissing Miller *was* better than sex with Jacob. Sure, he had a big dick, but it didn't mean he knew how to use it. He truly was incredible at oral, though.

But if Miller does anything half as well as he kisses, Jacob doesn't stand a chance against him. Just having his hands wrapped around my waist...feeling him against me...having his lips pressed tight against mine... It was all so much better than anything I've ever had before, and that scares me.

He was worth an A+ and more.

"I still can't believe you said yes to a date with him," Stevie says. "I mean, kissing him is one thing, but dating? That's a whole different beast."

"Sigh. Beast." Rosie fans herself, thinking of Rhodes. "Why are all the hockey players so damn hot?"

I don't know, but it's very distracting.

"It's just one date," I mumble, but I know it's more than that.

It's going to be my first date in three years after losing my dad and my long-term boyfriend all in one month. It's a huge step. I know it, and Stevie does too.

"Besides, who knows if this is even going to become a

thing? He could take me out and realize he's way out of my league."

"Or he could take you out and realize you're the love of his life."

I snort out a laugh. "Right. Sure. We'll both keep dreaming about that one."

"Stop selling yourself short, Scout," Stevie says with the big-sister authority in her voice that I've come to know over the years. "Not just to Miller, but to yourself too. You're a freaking catch, and any guy would be lucky to have you."

I give her a weak smile. "Thanks, but you have to say that."

"Well, I don't." Rosie waves her hand, then points to Stevie. "And I happen to agree with her. Who knows what could happen with Miller, but you can't write it off before you even try. I've done that before and totally shot myself in the foot. Now the guy I was in love with is madly in love with someone else. I blew my chance. Don't blow yours."

I'm surprised by her statements and also so curious to know what happened. I figure if she wanted to talk about it, she'd elaborate more, so I let it go.

"Okay," I say with a nod. "I'll give it a chance."

"And if nothing else, you'll have some great inspiration for your book." Stevie shrugs.

Hmm. She does have a good point there. I was feeling very inspired after Miller's kiss.

Maybe this *could* be good for my writing.

And…maybe for me too.

But I'm not going to get my hopes up. After all, this is Miller we're talking about—no way he's about to fall in love with little old me.

When Miller told me to wear a dress and heels, I figured we'd be going out to dinner.

What I didn't plan for was him taking me to the same place he's taken all the other dates he's been photographed with.

It's safe to say the reason my stomach feels like it's doing flips is not that I'm nervous—it's that I'm mad. I'm mad because there was a tiny part of me that hoped Stevie was right, hoped things with Miller were different, hoped maybe I was different.

But I'm just like all the rest…temporary.

I guess I know where I stand now.

"This place is nice, huh?" Miller says, reaching into the basket of bread and holding a piece my way. I shake my head, and he shrugs, not picking up on how clearly uncomfortable I am. "It's one of my favorites."

Oh, I'm aware.

But I don't say that. Instead, I tell him, "It's nice."

He scarfs down a piece of bread, then reaches for another.

I've yet to touch any or the glass of wine that's sitting

in front of me, which really says something because I *love* wine.

Silence falls over us, and it's not that comfortable, soothing kind.

It's awkward as hell. I know it, and Miller finally sees it too.

"Is, uh, something wrong?"

"Nope."

Except even I hear in my voice that something is definitely wrong.

He sets his bread down, swallows what's in his mouth, then chugs half his water. He reaches up and squeezes the back of his neck, massaging it for several seconds.

I remember that move. It's his tell.

He's nervous.

Now that I think about it, he was nervous on the way over here too, bouncing his leg as he drove entirely too fast. Hell, just sitting here now, he's buttoned and unbuttoned his suit jacket three times.

Why is he so nervous?

After another heavy minute of silence, he finally blows out a breath, then says, "I'm sorry. I shouldn't have brought you here."

"Oh?"

He sighs. "I won't lie, I've been on a lot of dates since I joined the Comets. It's kind of a thing I'm known for, being a serial dater."

You don't say.

"But there's a reason for it. I've never told anyone

this before. Well, besides Greer, and I'm not so sure he really counts. I mean, he's Greer. He's like the biggest asshole on the planet, but not really. That's just a front. I think he got his heart broken once upon a time, and now he's working on his villain origin story or something. He's…"

Miller's rambling. He's rambling because he's nervous. Why is he so nervous? It's not like we haven't been out together before. Sure, this is a little different because it's an actual, definite date, but it's still just me and him.

This is a stall, and I'm tired of waiting.

"…he became our number one goalie last year and—"

"No offense, Miller, but I really don't care about Greer."

He gives me a tight, shaky smile. "Right. Sorry." He clears his throat. "Look, the truth is I—"

"Is there anything else I can get you while you wait for your dinner?" the waiter asks, choosing that exact moment to appear beside the table. He gazes down at us with a saccharine smile. "Perhaps some more water, sir?"

Miller sets his now empty glass down, wiping his mouth with the back of his hand. "More water would be great. Or something stronger. Vodka? A big glass. On the rocks. No, wait—no rocks, just vodka. Lots of vodka. Two, please."

"Sure thing. Would you like some more bread? Maybe some of our delicious butter and oils to dip it in?

We have truffle oil, sweet garlic butter, and extra virgin olive oil that's—"

"Virgin!"

I'm not the only person who whips my head Miller's way at his outburst. No less than three tables in our vicinity turn, tuning in to our conversation.

"Uh, sir?" our waiter asks, now looking deeply concerned.

And I don't blame him because *What the fuck?*

I'm trying to catch Miller's gaze, but he's refusing to look at me. All he's doing is staring down at his plate, not looking at anyone.

"The olive oil, please," he mutters.

"Right away, sir." The waiter gives me a tight smile before walking away, looking over his shoulder a few times and shaking his head.

Miller continues staring at his plate, and eventually, the onlookers get tired of waiting for something else to happen and go back to their dinners.

"Miller?" I say quietly when he doesn't move for at least thirty seconds.

He sucks in a breath, then finally drags his eyes to mine. I've never seen his cheeks so red before, which is saying something because he's done and said plenty of embarrassing things in my presence.

But this is something else.

"Are you okay?" I ask gently.

"Virgin," he says again, his tongue darting out to wet his lips. "I'm a virgin, Scout."

CHAPTER 12

Oh fuck. Fuck, fuck, fuck.

This is it. We're done. Before we even had a chance to begin, Scout and I are done.

Why the hell did I just blurt out *virgin*? What the hell is wrong with me?

She's just staring at me with her jaw dropped, her eyes wide. She's thinking of bolting. I can see it. She probably thinks something is wrong with me or that I'm a total loser or—

"Okay."

I rear back because there is no way she just said what I think she said.

"Huh?"

"I said, *okay*. Is that not what you want me to say?"

"No. I…"

Well, shit. I actually don't know what I want her to say. Do I want her to be okay with this? Yes, because it's not a big deal to me. But do I just want her to say okay…? I don't know. I think really, I just want to know what she's thinking about.

I sit up higher in my chair, leaning over the table and keeping my voice low. "Does it bother you?"

She shakes her head. "Not one bit. Should it?"

"I guess not, no."

"Are you telling me because you want me to take your virginity?"

Fucking hell.

My face is on fire. I can feel the flames licking at my cheeks, can feel the sweat beginning to bead.

Scout take my virginity?

Well, I definitely don't hate the idea of that.

She laughs. "I'm kidding."

"But what if I did?"

All the humor drains from her face, and she looks just as surprised as I am by my words.

Do I mean them? *Is* that what I want? I don't know.

"I mean, I'm not saying no…"

She giggles. "Then I won't say no either."

"Okay."

I settle back in my seat, reaching for my glass of water, only to remember at the last minute that it's empty. My nerves are shot, and my throat feels like I swallowed an entire box of nails. I'm pretty sure if I stood right now, my legs would give out.

Where the hell is the waiter? I'm sure I scared him off by screaming *virgin* at him, but I need a drink—*stat.*

Silence engulfs us. All Scout can do is stare at me, and all I can do is look anywhere but at her.

This dinner is awful. I ruined everything.

God, I'm such an idiot.

When I finally peek up, Scout's head is tipped to the side, and she's watching me closely. A piece of hair has fallen loose from the braid that's lying over her shoulder, and I want to reach across the table and pull it between my fingers to see if it's as soft as it looks. I want to drag her closer to me and kiss her, or just sit with her and talk for hours.

What I definitely don't want is to sit in this damn restaurant for another minute.

Screw the drink. Screw the dinner. Screw this place.

"Do you want to get out of here?"

She nods enthusiastically. "Yes. Please."

"Good. I know just the place."

My chair scrapes loudly across the floor as I stand, drawing several eyes our way. It's the same people whose stares I felt earlier, and I can't say I'm bothered by them.

The waiter appears with my vodkas. I grab the glasses off his tray and set them on the table next to us.

"For your troubles," I tell the women who I heard mention were on their first date. "I hope it goes better than the one I'm on."

They both laugh, then pick the glasses up and clink them together before throwing them back in one gulp.

"We're leaving," I tell the waiter, digging my wallet from my back pocket and plucking out three one-hundred-dollar bills. I toss them onto his tray. "This should cover our bill."

His wide eyes land on the pile of cash, and all he can do is nod because that covers our dinner and then some.

"Thank you, sir. I hope you have a lovely evening."

He turns on his heel and walks away.

I look down at Scout, who is watching me with an amused grin, and extend my hand toward her.

"You ready?"

She slips her hand into mine. "Lead the way."

We pull into the parking lot of the gas station.

"Is this the place you know?"

"Nah. We're just here for snacks. I'm sure you're probably hungry since we didn't eat dinner, and I nervous-ate all the bread."

"Yes! I'm starving."

She throws the door open before I can tell her to wait, but I'm not surprised by it anymore. Scout's going to do what Scout's going to do, which is why I like her so much.

She's just...Scout.

She's entirely her own person, doing her own thing. She doesn't put on a front or pretend to be someone she isn't just so people will like her more. After growing up in the world I did with the parents I had where all they did was pretend, it's nice to have someone real.

I shuffle past her, at least holding this door open for her.

"Drinks or snacks first?"

"Snacks. Drink always depends on snack. You have to make sure they pair well together."

"Hm. I like the way you think."

We head for the snack aisle. She instantly grabs a packet of Reese's Pieces, snags peanut butter M&M'S next, and then selects a packet of Sour Skittles and some sour gummies.

"That's quite the jump," I comment.

"The Skittles and gummies are for me, the rest for you."

"For me?"

She nods. "You love peanut butter, right? That's why you always get the Chocolate Nutty Butter."

I don't know why I'm surprised she's caught on that I have a weird love affair with peanut butter, but I like that she noticed. "I fucking love peanut butter."

She grins. "I figured. Which means your drink is…" She leads us to the cooler section, perusing them until she finds just what she's looking for. She pops the door open, reaches in, and hands me a glass bottle. "A Yoo-hoo."

"A Yoo-hoo, huh?"

"Yep."

I grab the bottle, reading the label. "So, it's chocolate water?" My nose scrunches up. "Yeah, I don't know about that. Can't I just have chocolate milk instead?"

"Wait a minute—you've never had a Yoo-hoo before?"

I shake my head. "No. I wasn't really allowed sweets as a kid. It didn't fit in with my hockey routine."

Her jaw drops, and I slip a finger under her chin, pushing it back up.

"I can't believe you're twenty-four and have never had a Yoo-hoo."

"I've never had sex either."

"Miller!" A laugh bursts out of her, drawing the attention of the two other people in the store, but she doesn't care, and screw it—I don't care either.

I shrug. "It's true."

"I know." She closes the cooler, then moves down two more before swinging the door open and plucking out a root beer. It's the same thing she ordered when we had pizza. I wonder if it's her favorite and she would have gotten it no matter what snacks she picked.

"Is that all? We're just having candy?"

She screws her face up. "No. This is just our appetizer." She dips her head toward the island in the middle of the store. "We're having nachos."

So, we make nachos. At a freaking gas station. It's safe to say this date has definitely gone in a different direction than I originally planned.

We take our items to the register, where she adds two scratch-off lottery tickets to our pile.

Candy, nachos, and drinks in hand, we slip back into the car. Scout reaches over and turns on the radio as I pull out of the parking lot. I can't help but laugh at what's on and turn the Taylor Swift song up to full blast.

I head east, knowing just where I want to take us. Five minutes later, we're pulling into the parking lot of an old, run-down drive-in theater.

"What are we doing here? Didn't this place close a few years back?"

I don't answer her as I park the car in the middle of the lot directly in front of the old screen that's still up. There's a tear down the center, probably from some local high schoolers, and weeds almost as tall as the front of the car are sticking up out of the cracks in the pavement.

"I can't believe how much it's changed in two years. It's like the theater never even existed."

"You used to come here?"

I nod. "Back when I first joined the Comets, yeah. Only made it a few times before it shut down, but I always loved it."

She looks out at the vacant lot, a wistful look in her eye. "I used to come here with my dads all the time. Sundays were family days, which usually meant a movie or bowling. Stevie would always pick bowling, but I always wanted to go to the movies." She looks over at me with a smile. "For the stories, of course. Pops loved it too."

"Tell me a story, then."

"What? No way."

"Yes way." I point to the bag sitting at her feet. "But first, hand me that bag. I need my snacks for this."

"I'm not telling you a story," she says, but she hands me the bag anyway. I fish out my peanut butter treats along with my Yoo-hoo, then drop her sour candies onto the center console and set her root beer in the cup holder.

I open my mouth.

"Umm…" she says, staring at me.

"Nacho me."

"I am not feeding you, Miller."

"How rude." I pluck a chip from the plastic container, then another for good measure. "This is going to be awful with my chocolate water."

"Oh, disgusting for sure." She pops a chip into her mouth, moaning as she chews. "How is it something so cheap and what should be absolutely awful tastes so good?"

I shrug. "It's the way of life, I guess."

"I suppose."

I rip open my M&M'S, tossing a handful back. They taste terrible with the cheese from the nachos. I twist open the Yoo-hoo and take a tentative sip.

"Well?" she asks.

"It's not…bad. But it's not great either."

"Just wait. You're going to be addicted to them."

"We'll see." I take another drink, already liking it more. I cap the bottle, then set it back in the cup holder. "Enough stalling. Story time."

"You can't be serious."

"Oh, I am. You're a writer, aren't you? A storyteller?"

"Yes. No. I mean, I want to be."

"So, tell me a story, then."

"Miller...this is so embarrassing."

"More embarrassing than me yelling *virgin* in the middle of a restaurant where the average plate costs a hundred bucks?"

"Mine was only forty," she mumbles. "I ordered a salad."

"And you're still stalling."

"I totally am." She sighs. "All right, fine. Once upon a time..."

I push my seat back and settle down into my seat as she launches into a fairy tale about an American high schooler who finds out she's royalty. She gets sent to a foreign country to learn how to be part of the aristocracy, and at first, it's a disaster, but in the end, she winds up winning the hearts of everyone around her.

The way she tells it...it's enchanting, and I can't look away from her. The details are astounding, making it feel like I've been transported to this magical country and *I'm* the fucking princess.

By the time she's finished, I've eaten all of my M&M'S and half my bag of Reese's Pieces, and my chocolate water—which I admittedly love—is gone. I'm so invested that when she says *The End*, there are actual tears in my eyes—not that I'd ever admit that shit out loud.

"Wow. That was...incredible. Is that something you wrote?"

She cocks her head to the side, wrinkling her nose. "No, Miller. That's the plot of *The Princess Diaries*."

"Wait…so it's already a book?"

"Well, yes, but it's also a Disney movie. Have you never seen it?"

"Can't say I have."

"I was wondering why you just let me keep going. Your face when you found out she went down the stairs on a mattress was priceless."

"Because she's a princess!"

She tosses her head back in laughter, her entire body shaking. I don't even care that she's making fun of me right now. I love seeing her like this, so carefree and relaxed.

After several moments, she wipes at her eyes, exhaling sharply. "Wow. I needed that laugh."

"Long week?"

"Weird week." She nibbles at her bottom lip. "It was strange not having you around. It threw me off."

I grin. "I knew you liked me."

She rolls her eyes. "You wish."

"I do. Like you, I mean."

She peers over at me. "You do?"

"Yes. Very much."

The moonlight is bright enough that I don't miss the way her cheeks pinken at my admission.

"You're not what I was expecting, Miller."

"The virgin thing?"

Her eyes widen for a brief moment. "Well, that too. Can we…talk about that?"

"What's there to discuss?"

"Everything! Was I your first kiss?"

I laugh lightly. "No. That would be Abby Albertson in the eighth grade."

"Well, that's a relief, I guess. And…other stuff?"

"Are you asking me about my sexual history, Scout?"

"No!" Another deep blush. "Well, sort of, I suppose."

"I've done things, just not everything."

"I haven't done everything either. Like butt stuff—I haven't done that." What she's just blurted out hits her, and she sinks lower into her seat, covering her face with her hands. "Oh god. Kill me now."

"Nah. I kind of like you." I reach over, pulling her hands down. I grab her chin, tilting it my way. "I want to keep you around."

"You do?"

"Yeah. Do you still want to keep me around? With the virgin thing, I mean."

"Of course! It doesn't bother me at all. I'm just curious *how*."

"It's really the lamest answer of all time."

"Try me."

"Hockey."

"Huh?"

"Hockey." I lift my shoulders. "I was playing hockey. It was my life. Everything was about the game. I didn't do any of the normal teenage stuff because I wasn't allowed to. The only thing that mattered was making it pro, and after I did, it was about making it last." I swallow down the frustration that's settling into my stomach. "The longer it went on, though, the harder it became, and then I didn't want it to be with someone random. I...I wanted it to matter. I still want it to matter."

Now it's my face that's turning red because it's embarrassing. Guys aren't supposed to care about who they have sex with. It's socially acceptable for us to just bang and not give a crap, but that's not who I am or how I'm wired. And I'm finally starting to accept that.

She gives me a small smile. "That's not lame, Miller. It's unexpectedly sweet."

"Yeah? You don't think I'm a total loser?"

"Not at all. I think you're the exact opposite of that."

Relief floods me because her words seem genuine, and I like having genuine people in my life.

"Have, uh, have you really never told anyone before?"

I shake my head. "Just Greer. There's never really been anyone I've trusted."

"But you trust me?"

I nod. "I do. Do you trust me?"

It's her turn to nod. "I do."

"Good."

Then, I claim her mouth with mine.

She lets out a soft gasp, but it quickly turns into a low moan when my lips press against hers. I grip her waist, tugging her as close as I can in the confined space. Her hands find my hair, doing the same. This kiss is different from our last. It's rougher and faster, more desperate, like we've both been dying for it since the moment our lips last touched.

I wish we weren't in my car so I could properly feel her against me, so I could rake my hands over her whole body and touch every damn curve she has. She groans against my mouth like she's just as frustrated as I am by our lack of room to maneuver.

I might not be able to haul her into my lap, but that doesn't mean I can't touch her. I slide my hand from her waist and over her stomach. I feel her tense for only a moment when I do this, but she relaxes when she realizes my destination is much lower.

When my fingers collide with her bare thighs, I'm so damn thankful she's wearing a dress. She's warm and soft, and I have a feeling being between her legs would feel like heaven.

I snake my hand under her dress, fingering the hem of the silky material. Her legs fall apart like she's giving me permission to continue, and I don't hesitate to seize the opportunity. She sighs when I drag a single knuckle against her already soaked panties. She arches into my touch, wanting more when I run my fingertip over the edge of them. And then, when I finally slip my finger underneath the material, she gasps.

"Please…" she whispers against my lips.

"Please what, Scout? What do you want?"

"Touch me." It's not a request, not really. It's a demand—one I am more than happy to oblige.

I slide one finger over her clit, and she shivers. I do it again. Another shiver. This time a moan.

I tease and tease, knowing exactly what I'm doing when she's panting in my ear.

"Grady…"

My name rolling off her lips drives me mad, and I can't hold back any longer. I slant my mouth over hers just as I slide a finger into her, stroking her softly and slowly as I continue to brush my thumb against her clit.

She groans when I slide my finger out, only for it to turn into a low whimper when I dive back in with two, curling them up and finding the spot that has her bucking her hips off the seat.

She grips my forearm, holding me to her as she grinds against me. She's fucking my fingers now, riding the wave that's coursing through her.

"Oh god… I'm…" She cries out as she falls apart, gasping for air.

Tremors run through her body, and her nails dig into me, so rough I'm sure there will be a mark tomorrow, but I don't care. I've never witnessed anything so damn sexy before as she falls apart in my arms.

I kiss her again, trailing my lips from hers and across her jaw, down her neck, and back up again until I reach her mouth once more, placing one final kiss there before pulling away.

She slumps back against her seat, looking absolutely

drained in the best of ways. Her hair is a wreck, and there's a sheen of sweat across her forehead.

I can't help but laugh.

"What?" she asks, sounding so damn tired.

"Nothing. You just look adorable right now."

She scrunches her nose. "Adorable? I'm not sure anyone has ever called me that before."

"Well, they should, because it's true."

She lets out a soft yawn, covering her mouth with her hand. "Sorry."

"Don't apologize. I've clearly worn you out."

"And we didn't even have sex. Impressive."

"Does this mean I've earned myself an A-plus yet?"

"Not quite."

"Damn. I'll just have to try again on the second date."

She lifts her brows. "Second date, huh?"

"Or the third." I shrug. "I'm willing to go as many times as needed for a perfect grade."

"Don't go getting too ahead of yourself." She pats my cheeks. "Let's see how date two goes first."

I've never looked forward to a second date so much in my life.

CHAPTER 13

MILLER & SCOUT

Miller: I got a boner in the shower tonight.

Scout: That's…information I wasn't aware I needed.

Miller: Well, it's your fault, so that's why I thought you needed to know.

Scout: How is it my fault? You're hundreds of miles away!

Miller: Yeah, but I can't stop thinking about you and what happened in my car the other night.

Scout: Oh.

. . .

Miller: Yeah, oh.

Miller: It's very inconvenient, too. You're not supposed to get boners in the shower. That's like the number one locker room rule.

Scout: I'm sorry?

Miller: You should be. It's rude.

Miller: But it was totally worth it.

Miller: Is it inappropriate if I say I can't wait to do it again?

Scout: You literally just texted me about your boner. I think we're past inappropriate at this point.

Miller: That's fair.

. . .

Miller: Was that too much? I've been told I overshare sometimes.

Scout: No. It made me laugh, which I needed today.

Miller: Uh-oh. Bad day?

Scout: Just tired. I didn't get much sleep last night then had a cranky customer this morning that made me cranky.

Miller: Punch 'em in the nuts next time.

Scout: It was a lady.

Miller: Then punch her in the balls. Clearly, she's got 'em if she's getting sassy with you. You're kind of scary.

Scout: Oh?

Miller: Yeah. But it's in a hot way.

. . .

Scout: There's a hot way to be scary?

Miller: Of course there is.

Miller: There's like this fine line between scary and hot, which gives you scary hot.

Scout: No, right. That makes total sense.

Miller: It's not crazy.

Scout: I didn't say it was.

Miller: You have this...tone.

Scout: It's text. Can you really tell a tone in text?

Miller: YES!

. . .

Miller: ^That was exasperation.

Scout: Noted.

Miller: Do you miss me yet?

Scout: Not a chance.

Miller: Whatever you have to tell yourself, Scout.

Scout: *rolls eyes*

Scout: Go play hockey, Miller.

Scout: I thought you'd like to know that Macie was quite proud of your goal last night. She talked about it all throughout breakfast this morning.

Miller: She's proud of it? I'M proud of it! That was a fucking wicked shot!

. . .

Scout: There's that modesty you're known for.

Miller: Hey, someone's gotta toot my horn.

Scout: That...sounded oddly sexual.

Miller: I mean, it wasn't, but I like where your head is at.

Miller: Is this the start of phone sex?

Scout: WHAT? No! That's not at all what I meant!

Miller: Are you sure?

Scout: Very, very sure.

Miller: Boo!

. . .

Miller: But I respect your decision and will not pressure you.

Scout: Such a gentleman.

Miller: I do my best.

Miller: Any ideas for our second date tomorrow?

Scout: Nope. I'm not planning it. It's all on you.

Miller: Well, I have some ideas.

Miller: Naked ideas.

Miller: *waggles brows*

Scout: How did I know that was coming?

. . .

Miller: Because I'm me and whether you want to admit it or not, you like me and pay attention to me.

Scout: That's a stretch.

Miller: You liked me in my car when I had my fingers between your legs.

Scout: Can't stop thinking about it?

Miller: Can you?

Scout: No.

Miller: Are you blushing right now?

Scout: A little.

Miller: I like it when you blush.

· · ·

Miller: I especially like it when I'm the one to make you blush.

Scout: I've picked up on that.

Miller: Just think, I've been holding back too. Wait until you get to know me even better.

Scout: That kind of scares me a bit, I won't lie.

Miller: Nothing to fear.

Miller: Well…there's that one thing.

Scout: What one thing?

Scout: Miller?

Scout: MILLER?

· · ·

Scout: What one thing????

Scout: Oh. You're screwing with me, aren't you?

Miller: Guess you'll have to find out later.

Scout: You're so annoying.

Miller: You love it.

Scout: That's one way to describe it.

Miller: Tomorrow at four?

Scout: You know where to find me.

CHAPTER 14

SCOUT

Miller's fingers must be magic because in the last week since our date, I've written ten chapters.

And I haven't deleted a single one.

It's safe to say at this point he's my muse. After we kissed for the first time, I wrote. After the other night in his car, I *really* wrote. I can't stop thinking about my book, and the urge to write has never been stronger. I know it's all because of Miller and the way being with him makes me feel—*alive*.

He hasn't been around in three days thanks to the season starting, but we're still texting all the time. We haven't yet gotten a chance to go on our second date— that's tonight—and I am more than looking forward to it.

I've never really been one to fool around on the first date, but when Miller slid his fingers up my legs, it was like my body just knew what it wanted—him. And oh, man, was it right. I still can't shake the feeling of him between my thighs, can't get over the way I fell apart around him. The way he stroked me gently and kissed me so damn tenderly while I came down from my high…

He might be a virgin, but he's no fool. He knows exactly what he's doing.

To say I was shocked when he confessed his virginity to me would be an understatement. That was the absolute last thing I thought he was going to say. It doesn't seem real. How can he be twenty-four, a professional hockey player, *and* a virgin? Women throw themselves at him constantly. I've seen it with my own eyes, for crying out loud!

When he told me his reasoning, part of me felt bad for him because it's obvious he struggles with missing out on so many "normal" things because of his dedication to hockey. I mean, he's glad it all paid off, but I can see where that could be hard sometimes. He'd never even had a Yoo-hoo until the other night at the drive-in.

That was another surprise—there was no way he could have known what that place meant to me when he pulled into the abandoned lot, which made it all that much sweeter that he chose it.

I used to love the drive-in for my own reasons, but now…now I love it for others.

I clench my thighs together for probably the fifth time today.

"Aunt Scout! Miller is here!" Macie calls from the common area, which she and Stevie are currently cleaning up.

"What?!"

I poke my head out of the truck window, and sure enough, Miller *is* here.

Well, not technically *here* here.

He's currently across the street, sitting up on a stone ledge. Next to him is Eddie, who is waving his hands in the air, talking fast. He must be telling some story because Miller has his head thrown back in laughter. They look like two old friends catching up.

A smile overtakes my face at the sight of them together.

Most people would turn their nose up at Eddie. Hell, I've witnessed assholes driving by and yelling obscenities out their windows at him, some truly vile things.

Then you have Miller, a hotshot hockey player taking five minutes out of his busy day to treat this man like the human being he is.

I'm so glad he's not an asshole.

Almost as if he can sense I'm thinking about him, he turns his head and looks my way.

I see the grin that fills his face, and he elbows Eddie, then nods toward me. Eddie turns his attention in my direction, then says something to Miller. I wish like hell I could read lips from this far away because his grin grows wider as he nods, agreeing with whatever Eddie said to him.

Miller pats Eddie on the back and gets up, heading toward the truck.

I busy myself with work as he saunters—and I really do mean saunters—over. I may act like I'm not paying him any attention, but from the smirk on his face, he knows I am very much tuned in to what he's doing.

He sends a wave to Macie and Stevie as he makes his way up to the window.

"Hey," he says casually when he reaches the truck.

"Um, hi. Did I get the time of our date wrong?" I ask.

"Nope. We're still on for four. I was just coming by to see Eddie."

"Do you hang out with him often?"

I've seen Miller talking with him several times over the years. He always buys him donuts and coffee, and they sit on the wall or along the sidewalk.

"I try to stop and see him at least weekly, sometimes more often if I can find him. He moves around to a few different places, but since I come here so often, I try to check up on him here."

"How'd you meet him?"

He lifts a shoulder. "He was here. I was here. We just started talking. We've been friends since. I've tried to get him off the streets a few times, but he refuses, and I'm not going to push it. But during the winter, when it gets cold, I make him at least let me pay for a hotel so he can warm up."

"That's sweet of you, Miller."

His brows furrow. "It's not sweet. It's basic human decency."

"Trust me, not every person is decent like that. The things I've heard people say to him..."

His face darkens. "Let me catch one asshole saying shit to him. Wright won't be the only one to get arrested on our team."

"Oh my gosh. I almost forgot about that."

It happened just a few weeks after the Comets lost in the Finals in one of the worst ways ever. It was all over the news, and people were worried Wright was going to get shipped to a different team, but he didn't. He stayed and came back better than ever the following year.

"Need any help cleaning up?" he asks, looking around at the mess I'm still working on.

Sundays are always our busiest days, and this one was no exception. The line was out of the parking lot at one point, and it just seemed to get bigger and bigger. I'm about eighty percent sure it's because we brought back the Comets Cosmic Brownie donut for the start of the season, and fans were hoping a player would be here. I wanted to ask Miller to stop by, but given how much we've been hanging out lately, it felt weird cashing in a favor like that.

"I think I'm about done. Macie and Stevie are working on the tables now, and I'm almost finished in here. I was going to run home and clean up first. I most definitely need a shower."

"Or…" he says. "You can shower at my place."

I lift my brows. "Your place?"

He nods. "I was thinking maybe I can make you dinner."

I was not expecting that. "You cook?"

"A little. Not much." He blows out a breath. "All right, fine. I was going to boil noodles, throw some jar sauce on top, and call it good."

I wrinkle my nose. "No. That will not do. How about *I* cook, and you can make a salad?"

"I feel like that's not fair. You've been working all day."

"I don't mind. It'll be a nice break from making sweets."

"We can run by the store after you're done here and grab ingredients if you want? We can stop by your place and grab clothes for tomorrow."

He says it so causally like he didn't just skip over the many hours we still have left in the day.

Does this mean…

"I've never had a slumber party either," he says. "Figured since we're checking some things off my list, like Yoo-hoos, maybe try that one too. Plus, I'm leaving for an extended away trip soon. If you stay over, we could maybe even get a third date in before I go."

I feel like it should scare me, like I shouldn't be staying at his place so soon. I wait for the little voice in my head that says it's a bad idea and we should take it slow.

But it never comes.

I'm not sure how I feel about it, but before I can analyze it, Stevie says, "She'll stay!"

"Stevie!" I yell at her.

"What?" She shrugs. "I've totally been listening in the

whole time. You should stay at his place." She looks at Miller. "And it's really weird that you've never had a Yoo-hoo before."

"Don't judge."

"And stop listening in!" I add.

She walks away with her hands in the air like she's innocent when we all know she's far from it. She's probably just going somewhere else to hide and listen.

Miller looks back at me. "Don't let her pressure you. If you don't want to stay over, you don't have to. It's not like I'm *expecting* anything, if you catch my drift."

I do catch it, and I appreciate it. But...I actually think I'd be okay if something did happen. I didn't realize how dormant I've felt in the last three years, and now that I've had an orgasm that didn't come from my vibrator, I want more.

"I can do a slumber party," I tell him.

"Yeah?" I nod. "Cool." He leans closer. "And, Scout?"

I inch forward. "Yes?"

"Maybe don't pack any pajamas."

He shoves off the truck, spinning away and leaving me there with my mouth hanging open.

Stevie holds her hand up for a high five. "Nice."

He smirks...and taps his hand to hers.

For what feels like the hundredth time, I wonder what I've gotten myself into with Miller...and why I'm so excited about it.

"Do you want cheese on the garlic bread?"

"Yes, please."

I nod, grabbing a tub of grated parmesan. Normally I'd grate it myself, but I have no idea what kind of supplies Miller has at his place.

We look ridiculous walking through the store together right now. I'm still wearing my trusty overalls, and my hair is a chaotic mess. He's my exact opposite—put together in jeans and a nice t-shirt that looks entirely too soft and still has fold marks on it.

"Do you have extra virgin olive oil at home?"

"Among other types of virgins, yes."

"Miller!" I hiss.

"What? I meant you and butt stuff."

I shake my head, steering the cart toward the next item on our list.

When we get to the aisle with the tomato paste, I'm annoyed it's on the top shelf. Why do they have to put things so high?

I rise up on my tiptoes and reach for the jar, but I don't make it very far before Miller is there behind me. One hand goes to my waist, and his warmth washes over me as he reaches around, grabbing the jar with ease. My ass is lined up with his cock, and I don't miss the way he presses against me, making sure I feel every single inch of him.

Two can play that game.

I grind against him, adding friction to the fire he's trying to ignite.

He groans, and a deep growl moves through him. "Woman."

I laugh, ducking under his arm and squeezing around him. "What?"

"You're mean."

"Oh, *I'm* mean? You know exactly what you were just doing."

"Reaching for the jar you needed?"

"Uh-huh." I glance down at the bulge that's not so hidden in his jeans. "You know what they say, Miller: play stupid games, win stupid prizes."

"Oh, I have a prize for you…"

I let out a loud squeak as he stalks toward me with a spark in his eyes that's pure desire.

He doesn't stop until he has me pressed against the cart. He places his hands on it, caging me in like he's a predator and I'm his prey.

"I hope you know that once we get home, this game will continue…and you will lose."

"Is it really losing if I'm *satisfied* in the end?" I challenge with a lifted brow.

He narrows his eyes. "Who said I'm going to let you come?"

"I saw the look in your eye the other night, and I think you enjoyed your fingers between my legs as much as I did."

He knows I have him there. "You—"

"Hey, you creep! You leave that young woman alone!"

Miller whirls around, and I peek around him to find an old woman pointing a finger at us.

"I'm not—"

"OH MY GOD, HIS PENIS!"

Miller rushes toward her. "Ma'am! I—"

"Security! Security! He's trying to touch me with his penis!"

Then, the old woman starts screaming, and that's when all hell breaks loose.

"I can't believe she hit you, or that you went down."

"I can't believe she called security on me. I'm the one who was assaulted!"

"Well, you did point your boner directly at her…"

"A boner that was your fault!" He winces when I remove the ice pack from his face. There's a cut from the metal spikes on her purse and a pretty dark bruise has formed, but it's nothing too serious. "What the hell did she even have in her bag? That thing was heavy as hell."

"I'm pretty sure it was full of bingo daubers. I counted like twenty while we waited for management to sort it out."

"Seriously?"

I nod. "Seriously. And then she asked for your autograph after all of that."

He shakes his head. "I'm just glad nobody called the police."

"She threatened to."

"I didn't even do anything!"

He rises off his stool as he says this, but I shove him back down.

"I know," I say. "They know too. We got it all settled."

He groans. "God, Coach is going to flip when he hears about this tomorrow. And all the guys are going to laugh."

I giggle because it's hilarious when you think about it. Miller doesn't appreciate it, sending a stern glare my way, which in turn makes me laugh harder.

Eventually he cracks, and we're both laughing.

"You know," he says once we've settled down, "we're really not having a good track record with dates. The first one I…"

"Ruined it by screaming at the waiter about your virginity, and the second…"

"I ruined with my virgin wiener."

That sends us into another fit of laughter.

"I think I'm most upset we ended up leaving the store empty-handed because I was really looking forward to our dinner," Miller says.

"It's fine. We'll do it another night. Besides, I was kind of craving pizza anyway."

"I think we needed something easy after that chaos. It

should be here in about ten minutes if you want to go shower."

"Are you sure?" I ask, even though I really do want to wash up. I'm still a mess from working in the truck all day.

"Yeah," he says, taking the ice pack from my hands. "I'll be fine. My bedroom is down at the end of the hall. The bathroom is kind of hard to miss from there. I'll give you the grand tour after we eat."

"If you insist…" I hop off the stool and start heading that way, then realize my mistake. "Oh crap! We forgot to stop by my place for clothes. Now our slumber party is ruined."

"No. No way. We've already had enough things get ruined—this one won't be one of them. I'll find you something to wear."

I laugh. "Yeah, right. Your clothes aren't going to fit me, Miller."

He narrows his eyes. "I'll find you something and set it on the bathroom counter."

I want to argue because there is just no way he's going to find anything that'll cover everything, but he's already had a hard enough evening, so I don't.

"Okay. I'll be quick," I promise, heading off down the hall.

Miller lives in one of the big, swanky buildings downtown that overlooks the city, and his place is massive. Stevie and I could easily fit our entire apartment inside of his living room. I'm dying to peek around in every room, but I don't want to be nosy. I can't help myself when I get to his bedroom, though. I *have* to look around.

I don't know why, but to me, Miller always screamed a messy-frat-guy apartment. That's not the case at all. It's neat and tidy, and even his bed is made to perfection. I wonder if he has a cleaner come in or if he's just this organized himself.

There aren't any knickknacks lying around, just a book on the side table. I peek at the cover and burst out laughing when I see what he's reading: *The Princess Diaries* by Meg Cabot.

Of course that's what he's reading.

I set the book back down, then make my way into his bathroom. It's the same monochromatic scheme as the rest of the house, but the real beauty of the space is the massive walk-in shower. There's no door; you just walk right in, and there's a frosted glass window so you're not completely boxed in. Deep gray stonework covers every inch, and there's a black bench tucked in the back. It's easily the most gorgeous bathroom I've ever seen in person.

I strip, setting my dirty clothes near his hamper, then I turn on the water to let it heat up. Water spurts out from two different directions, and I giggle with glee because I already know this is going to be the best shower of my life.

Once the water is warmed up—which takes all of

twenty seconds—I step inside and literally groan with relief when the heat rushes over me.

I stand under the streams for several minutes before I even consider doing anything else. There's not much in the way of products in here—though that's not surprising —so I make do with what I have. I apologize to my hair for having to use the 2-in-1, then squirt some of his woodsy-scented body wash into my hands.

I freeze when I hear the door creak open and then remember it's just Miller bringing me clothes, and I relax. I know he can't really see, just the outline, but I can still feel his eyes on me. My immediate reaction is to be embarrassed by this, but I can't bring myself to actually feel that way, not when I can feel his stare dancing along my body as I rinse the soap away.

There's a part of me that wants to invite him into the shower, wants to haul him to me and kiss him senseless… but I'm not sure I'm ready for that quite yet.

Based on the fact that the soap is long gone by the time he makes the decision to leave the bathroom, he's thinking about it too.

Once he's gone, I shut the water off and grab the nearest towel to dry off.

"Oh god." I moan, slipping it around my body. "Even the freaking towels are amazing."

I notice my dirty clothes are gone, and sitting on the counter are the replacements.

I laugh when I pick them up. "He's insane. This won't fit."

I'm proven wrong when I pull the shirt over my body, and not only does it fit, but there's also still room. It hits mid-thigh, which is good because I have no underwear and the pair of shorts Miller left won't fit.

I run my fingers through my wet hair, fluffing it up a bit so I don't go out there looking like a drowned rat.

I look at myself in the mirror. I'm wearing a shirt that's just big enough to cover me, but if I lift my arms at all, all my goodies are going to hang out, and I look ridiculous with my wet hair. This is the best I can do given the situation, though.

The situation is I'm staying the night with Grady Miller.

Oh god. What the hell has my life turned into over the last month and a half? I went from working constantly and holing up at home when I had time off to having a sleepover with a hockey player.

Stevie said I needed writing inspiration, and this is some top-tier stuff. Maybe after whatever this is with Miller runs its course, I'll finally have a finished book.

A faint knock at the front door pulls me from my thoughts, and right on cue, my stomach growls because it knows it's pizza time.

With one last glance at myself, deciding there's not much else I can do, I take a deep breath and set out to find Miller.

CHAPTER 15

I'm fucked.

Not literally—though I wish.

But I'm totally screwed.

When I set clothes on the counter for her, I expected her to march out here in a towel and tell me she wasn't going to wear it. I didn't expect her to put it on, but now she's standing before me wearing the Comets logo across her chest with my name and number across her back.

It's hot as fuck.

"Thanks for the t-shirt," she says, yanking it down lower when it rides up a bit as she pads farther into the kitchen.

"T-shirt? You're killing me, woman. It's a jersey, or even a sweater—but definitely not a t-shirt."

"That's the second time you've called me that today."

I tip my head, unsure what she's meaning.

"Woman," she clarifies. "You said it in the grocery store too."

"Oh. Do you not like it?"

"Honestly, I didn't think I would, but…you keep growling it. It's kind of hot."

"I growl?"

"Yeah." She nods. "Like…*woman.*"

She drops her voice a few octaves, really pushing the word out from her chest, and I can't help but laugh.

"There's no way I sound like that."

"You do." She shrugs. "But it's okay because it's hot."

"Is it?"

"Oh yeah. Sometimes guys do that in romance novels, and I've always wondered what it meant and why it gets the heroine all hot and bothered, but then you…" She waves her hand toward me. "Yeah."

"Are you saying you're all hot and bothered right now?"

Pink colors her cheeks. "Well, I'm not *not* hot and bothered. It doesn't help that you stole my bra, and this *jersey* feels really good against my nipples." She slaps her hand over her mouth. "Oh my god. Forget I said that."

Oh, I cannot forget she said that. Not in a million years will I forget she said that.

Fuck. Just thinking about her nipples makes my dick throb.

To be fair, everything about Scout makes my dick throb. She just has this effortless sexiness about her that I find incredibly attractive.

"Please?" she asks, eyes still wide.

"Not a chance."

Before I know it, I'm crossing the kitchen and scooping her into my arms.

"Miller!" She squeals out a surprised laugh. "What the—put me down!"

"Fine," I say, placing her on the counter, just where I wanted her all along.

"You're insane," she says breathlessly as I step in between her legs.

"Maybe a little." I nuzzle my face into her neck, kissing her softly.

She's trembling in my arms—literally.

"Are you okay?" I ask.

"The counter is cold against my ass."

I pull my head back and look at her. "Against your…" It all clicks into place. "You're not wearing any underwear, are you?"

She sinks her teeth into her bottom lip, shaking her head just a little.

Even I hear the growl that leaves me this time.

I slide my eyes down her body and see that the jersey has ridden up into very dangerous territory. It's covering just the tippy tops of her thighs now. If she were to move even just an inch, it wouldn't be covering anything at all.

I really want her to move an inch.

I meet her gaze, and I'm not surprised to find she's staring at me with the same look that's probably in my eyes—unabashed need.

"Can I…see?"

A soft exhale leaves her lips, and she hesitates for only a moment before nodding softly. "Yes."

I don't waste a single second, don't give her any room to change her mind. I place my hands on her knees and spread them apart.

I was right about Scout—she's stunning.

But seeing her sitting on my counter with her legs spread and her pretty pink pussy on display? She's a fucking goddess.

I drop to my knees, ready to worship her as she deserves. I look up to find her watching me with heavy-lidded eyes.

"Can I try something?" I ask her.

Her eyes widen for only a moment. "You've never...?"

I shake my head once. "No."

"Oh. I'd be your...first?"

And hopefully my last.

I don't know where the thought comes from, but it slams into me all the same. I don't know if I like it or if I even want it to be true, but it doesn't necessarily feel wrong.

"Yes."

"Okay."

"Can you...tell me how you'd write it?"

"What?"

"Tell me how they do it in your books. I want this to be good for you. *I* want to be good for you."

She swallows thickly, and her chest heaves. I think she's going to say no, think she won't do it.

But then she says, "Kiss my thighs first." Another hard swallow. "The hero would kiss my thighs first."

So, I do. I press my lips to the spot just above her knee and kiss my way up, up, up until just before the haven between her legs. Then, I start again on the other leg. I repeat it over and over until she's squirming on the counter.

"Miller…" She crashes her fingers through my hair, tugging on the strands. "You're killing me."

"In a good way?"

"Yes, but I need more…"

"What next?"

"Taste me…" she begs. "Please."

She guides my head toward her pussy, and I'm happy to follow her instructions.

I flatten my tongue, sliding it against her, and now I'm the one making noises because *holy hell*. She tastes incredible. Sweet, just like I knew she would.

I do it again. And again. She tilts her hips, giving me better access as I continue to lavish her. Her moans fill the kitchen, and I swear if someone recorded it, I would listen to it all day.

"Suck my clit," she instructs.

I pull the little bud into my mouth, applying pressure, and she damn near flies off the counter.

"Oh god." Another moan. "Don't stop. Please."

I drag her even closer until she's teetering on the

edge, gripping my hair for leverage as I continue to suck and lick and tease her into oblivion. I do it not only because she loves it, but because I love it. I think I could move in here if she'd let me.

"I'm so close," she mutters. "So, so close."

And that's the last coherent thing that leaves her mouth as she trembles around me, her thighs squeezing me almost too tightly as she rides the waves of her orgasm on my tongue.

Her grip on my hair slowly loosens, and her legs relax. I know I need the air, but I almost don't want it. If this is how I go, it'll be the sweetest death of all time.

I give her one last kiss before sitting back, and I peer up at her. Her chest is rising and falling rapidly, her eyes still screwed tightly shut. There's a faint sheen of sweat along her forehead, but I swear she looks more relaxed than I've ever seen her before.

She peels her eyes open one at a time, then looks down at me.

"Well?" I ask, brow raised. "How'd I do?"

She laughs breathlessly. "I think you just earned that A-plus."

"You've never been to a hockey game before?"

She shakes her head. "Nope. I mean, I've watched plenty thanks to Macie, but I've never attended a live game."

"Well, we'll have to change that. You can come to one of mine, cheer me on." I tug at the jersey she's still wearing. "Maybe you can wear this. The number thirteen suits you."

Completely stuffed from the cold pizza we devoured, we're lounging on the couch, both refusing to move. Scout has her legs draped over my lap, and every time she wiggles around, I get to see what's underneath her shirt—nothing.

"I bet you say that to all the girls."

"You do remember our whole virgin conversation, right?"

"Well, yeah," she says, picking at her sleeve, not looking at me. "But I assume you've had girlfriends or girls at your games."

"No."

She slowly drags her eyes to me. "No?"

"You heard me. No, I've never had a girlfriend before, and I definitely don't bring random girls to my games like some guys in the league who hand their game tickets out to whatever puck bunny they find. That's not my style."

Her mouth forms an O. "You've never had a girlfriend?"

"I didn't go to prom or homecoming. I never missed a day of school or snuck out of the house or went to a frat party. I've also never had a job that wasn't hockey."

Her eyes grow bigger and bigger the longer the list

gets. "That's…wow. You weren't kidding when you said your entire life has been hockey."

"I really wasn't."

"Is that… How do you feel about it? Do you regret it?"

I wave my hand around my apartment, which costs a ridiculous amount of money. "It's kind of hard to sometimes." Keeping one hand on her leg, I squeeze the back of my neck with the other. I exhale a heavy breath. "But sometimes, yeah. I just feel like I've missed out on so much, you know? I hear stories from the other guys about goofy shit they used to do, but I don't have any stories like that. When I say my parents were dead set on me making it into the NHL, I mean it. They had my sister when they were young and broke. Then I came along, and they were really broke then. Until they realized I had skills. So, I became everything to them. I was their future, their retirement plan."

She doesn't say anything for several moments, and when I finally look over to check on her, I'm surprised to find her face red with anger.

"What?"

"That is the most fucked-up thing I've ever heard, Miller."

I laugh, though there isn't an ounce of humor in it. "It is pretty fucked up, huh?"

"Yes!" She shuffles around until she's sitting up more. "You're not a retirement plan. You're their fucking kid.

They should have never, ever done that to you. They took so much away."

"But they gave me a lot too."

"What? Money? That comes and goes. They should have let you be a kid, make stupid mistakes, experience things—not make your entire life about a game so they had something to fall back on. It makes me so mad."

"It makes me mad too."

"How's your relationship now that you are where you are?"

"The same as it's always been. When my career is riding a high, they're happy and leave me alone. But when I slip…that's when I hear from them, and it's just so they can tell me to be better."

She shakes her head in disgust. "I'm so sorry. You deserve better than that."

She's right; I do, but right now, it's not a battle I want to fight. Right now, I just want to find what makes me happy, and at this moment, it's Scout.

Before she can protest, I reach over and haul her into my lap until she's straddling me.

"Hi," I say once I have her right where I want her. Her mouth is mere inches from mine, and I want to devour it.

"Hi," she repeats with a smile. "What are you doing?"

"I'm changing the subject."

"Oh?"

"Yep. Anatomy. Wait, no—I meant sex ed."

She giggles. "Is that so?"

"Yes. I think I'm failing, and I need a tutor. Could you help?"

Scout wiggles, and I know there's no way she doesn't feel my very hard dick, which my sweatpants are concealing rather poorly.

"I think I can give you some pointers."

I drive my hips into her. "I can give *you* some pointers."

She pulls back, screwing her face up. "That was terrible."

I laugh, tugging her back to me and giving her a gentle kiss. "It really was. This is why I need help."

"Clearly."

"I'm willing to do whatever it takes to earn a passing grade. Maybe some extra credit?"

"Extra credit, huh?"

"Yes. Anything."

"Kiss me, then."

So, I do. Our pace is slow and sweet as I take my time with her, our tongues moving together in perfect rhythm. I slip my hands under the jersey, cupping her ass and massaging her cheeks as she grinds her hips against me.

Fuck. My cock is aching, *hurting* even. I need a release, and I need it badly. I've never felt like this before, like I could combust and never be the same again. I shouldn't be surprised, though—everything with Scout seems to feel different.

She dances her fingers under my shirt, lightly

dragging her fingernails over my abdomen. It feels good, but I want to feel more.

I break our kiss just long enough to strip my shirt from my body, then I pull her mouth back to mine. I try to bring her back toward me, but she shakes her head, shoving me back against the couch.

She tugs the jersey over her head.

And that's how Scout ends up naked in my lap.

She's gorgeous. Her deep brown hair is still a little damp from her shower, and I love the way it curls around her shoulders. Her cheeks are painted red from our kissing, and her eyes are glassy with desire.

Yeah, her stomach has rolls, there are stretch marks on her skin, and her hips and legs have dimples all over them, but I love every single fucking inch of her.

I reach out, dragging my finger across one of the deeper red marks on her belly. The first thought I have is dumb. *Does it hurt?* Of course it doesn't. Or maybe it does, just not in a physical way.

I continue tracing the others, then run my fingertips over the dimples on her legs. I do it not only because I love them, but because I want *her* to know I'm not bothered by them at all. She's made a few comments about her body and how she's not the "typical" woman I would date, whatever the fuck that means, and it pains me to think she would believe she's not enough for me just because of something silly like stretch marks or cellulite.

Her body is beautiful, but she's more than that. She's Scout, and that's what I like so much about her.

"Please say something," she whispers.

When I finally shift my eyes to her face, I see she's looking at me with worry in hers.

"Can I suck on your tits?"

A laugh bubbles out of her. "That was kind of the plan."

I don't waste a second, leaning forward and capturing one of her nipples between my teeth. She groans the second the tight, pink bud touches my tongue, and all I can think is, *I love it too, Scout.*

I play with her breasts, moving from one to the other, sucking and licking and kissing them until she's rocking against my painfully hard cock. There's an obvious wet spot forming on my sweats, and seeing how turned on she is right now is about to send me over the edge.

I grip her hips, stilling her movements because I'm about two seconds from embarrassing myself and need her to stop moving.

"No. No, no, no," she chants. "I need…"

"Scout, if you keep rubbing against me, I'm going to come in my pants."

Her eyes pop open, and I swear, based on the look in her eyes, she likes the idea of that.

"I want to see."

"What?"

"I want to see you come."

I've never jacked off in front of a girl before, and the

thought of doing it makes me momentarily nervous, but I don't care. I *need* to come, and if it's what Scout wants, I want it too.

I pull my sweats down as far as I can with her still on my lap, letting my cock spring free between us. She stares down at me, her tongue darting out of her mouth to wet her lips, liking what she sees.

Funny, because I'm liking what I see too—a naked Scout on my lap with her pussy drenching my thighs.

Unable to help myself, I reach out, slipping two fingers between her legs. She lets out a soft moan when I pump two fingers inside of her, running circles over her clit with my thumb.

But just as soon as she begins rocking against me, I remove them.

"Ugh, you're the worst. I—"

Her words die on her lips when she watches the hand that's coated in her move around my cock and begin to stroke.

"Oh god," she mutters, unable to look away.

I press my free hand against her lower belly and use my thumb to put pressure on her clit as she moves her hips in time with me. She can't take her eyes off me, and I can't take mine off her as I continue to stroke myself.

"I'm so close, Miller," she says, her breaths coming in sharper and sharper by the second. "So...*ahhh.*"

Her body convulses as she falls apart, and I feel it. The sight of her with her head thrown back, tits still on full display and red from the scratchiness of my beard is almost enough to send me over the edge.

"Shit, Scout. I'm going to come."

"Do it." She cups the back of my neck, scratching her nails along my skin. "On me. Do it on me."

I look up to make sure she's not joking—and she's not. Her eyes are glazed over, and her face is red and she's breathing hard, but there isn't an ounce of her that's kidding. I've never been more fucking turned on.

I watch her as she watches me, jacking myself until I'm spilling all over her stomach and tits.

Fuck me.

The sight of my cum on her is killing me because I love the idea of marking her up, claiming her, making her *mine*.

She reaches down, smearing her finger through a bit of it, playing with it.

Then I watch with absolute fucking delight as she drags her finger through the mess and licks it clean.

It's the hottest thing I've ever witnessed.

Not caring that she's just had me in her mouth, I crash my lips to hers, kissing her until we're both gasping for air.

When we finally break, she sags against me, not caring about the mess between us as we work to catch our breath. I might be an athlete with amazing stamina, but holy hell, I am tired right now. I feel like I could close my eyes and fall asleep.

I'm not sure how long we sit there or how many

strangled breaths we gasp in, but it's long enough for her to go quiet.

"Hey," I whisper, "are you asleep?"

She shakes her head, peeling herself off me and back up into a sitting position. There's a lazy grin on her face, which makes me grin.

"No. I'm just exhausted."

"Good exhausted?"

"Very, very good." Her smile grows wider. "Not bad for a first sleepover, Miller. Not bad at all."

CHAPTER 16

SCOUT

It's official: I can't stop smiling.

And it's all because of Miller.

We've been spending all our free time together. If he's not at the rink, he's here. If he doesn't have a game, I'm staying the night at his place, and he's giving me orgasms until the sun comes up.

I'm tired all the time, but even so, there is absolutely nothing that could knock this grin off my face right now.

"What's my baby girl smiling so hard about?"

I freeze in shock at the familiar voice. There's no way...

I look up, and yep, my father is standing outside of the truck. His graying hair is brushed back in its usual style, and he's wearing his famous tan khakis and polo shirt. Pops was always the more fashion-forward of the two, but he never pushed Dad to wear anything he didn't want to, so he didn't.

Meanwhile, I'm in here thinking about all the dirty

things I got up to last night with the pro hockey player I'm kind of dating.

"You're… Dad!"

He lifts his dark, bushy brows, laughing. "That'd be me. How's my girl doing?"

"Good. Great. Good." *Oh god.* Even I hear how high-pitched and surprised my voice is right now. "Great."

"That's good. Or should I say great?"

"Sorry," I say with a short laugh. "I'm a little tired and just wasn't expecting you, is all."

"What? An old man can't surprise his daughter at work?"

"Of course you can. I just…" I lift my gloved hands; they're covered in the filling for our Comets Cosmic Brownie donut, which is stuffed with brownie batter.

"I got that, boss," Rosie says, pushing me aside. "Go visit with your dad, and I'll finish these up."

I glance over at her. "Are you sure?"

"Of course. I just finished prepping the pudding for the Bananas Over You donut, so I need something new to do."

"Okay," I say, tugging my gloves off. "If you insist. Dad, you want a coffee or anything?"

"That'd be great, sweetie. And maybe a—"

"Cheery Cherry Cheesecake donut?"

He grins. "You know me so well. I'll go grab us a spot."

I toss my gloves away and wash my hands, then pour a hot black coffee for my father and make myself a vanilla cold brew. After grabbing us each a donut, I find him sitting at a table...and he's not alone.

"Miller!"

He turns at the sound of his name, spinning around to grin at me.

"Hey, thanks," he says, jumping up to grab the cold brew from my hands and smacking a kiss on my cheek. "How'd you know that's what I wanted?" He nods toward my father. "This guy was just telling me about how he's a huge Comets fan."

I'm frozen in place, my eyes wide as I meet my dad's very confused-slash-amused expression.

"Well," he says quietly, "this is quite the surprise."

You have no idea.

I shake my head, then walk forward, sliding his coffee across the table. I take a seat, and Miller slides in next to me.

"I see you two have already met, but I suppose a formal introduction is in order..." I look from my father to Miller. "Miller, this is my dad. Dad, this is..."

I trail off because I'm not entirely sure what to say about who Miller is to me. We're dating, but I'm not sure he'd be comfortable with me labeling him my boyfriend.

I settle on: "This is Grady."

"*The* Grady Miller," my dad says. "As in the Comets' Grady Miller."

"Yes," I confirm, even though I don't need to.

"Dad..." Miller's eyes grow about three sizes. He

gulps. "Oh." He wipes his hand on his pant leg, then extends it my father's way. "It's great to meet you, sir."

My dad eyes his hand warily, taking a sip from his coffee, flicking his gaze between me and Miller. "Hmm. When did this happen?"

Miller takes his hand back, laughing awkwardly. He looks nervous, and I can't say I blame him. Dad is a former firefighter and a big, burly guy. He's intimidating until you get to know him and find out he's just a big softy.

"Well, it's kind of a long story," Miller starts.

"I'm retired. I have time."

"Right." Another awkward chuckle from Miller. "We, uh, we've known one another for a while."

"You know the Comets come by here a lot," I add.

Miller nods. "Yeah, we love this place. It's one of our favorites. I met Scout here." He shakes his head. "No, wait—that's not true. I mean, it kind of is, but not."

I dare a peek at my father, who has his brows pinched tightly together, hanging on Miller's every word.

"I was an idiot, sir. I knew your daughter from the truck, but I didn't really *know* her. She wasn't on my radar. I screwed up and hurt her feelings, and it made me feel like absolute shit."

His face sours like he still feels that way just thinking about it.

"So," he continues. "I made it my mission to make it up to her." He shoots me a grin, and I can't help but smile back at him. "And after a lot of groveling and admitting what a moron I am, she forgave me. After spending so much time with her, I knew I would never forgive myself if I didn't do everything I could to extend it. So, I did. I asked her out, and, luckily, she said yes."

My dad looks at me, surprised by this. He knows what I went through with Aaron and how I've stayed single since everything went down with him. The fact that I'm dipping my toes back into the dating pool with a hockey player is mind-blowing to me too.

"It's still new," Miller tells him, resting his hand on my leg. "But I like her, sir." He gives me a gentle squeeze. "A lot."

I like you a lot, too.

It surprises me how true the words are. I'm trying hard not to get too attached to him. Sure, we're spending a lot of time together, but I keep reminding myself this is all new for him. He's never had a relationship before, and he's never done any of this. I'm not stupid enough to think he's going to stick around. He'll probably get his fill and leave me in the dust, ready for something else. I get it.

Besides, it's not like I'm not benefiting from this too, and I don't just mean orgasms. I wrote a whole new chapter this morning during my break. My inspiration is at an all-time high.

"Okay," my dad says, pulling my attention back to him.

"Okay?" Miller asks, looking at me for confirmation.

My dad shrugs. "Yeah. As long as you own up to your

mistakes and treat my daughter right from now on, okay. My partner…" He smiles wistfully, no doubt picturing his late husband. "He'd have loved how honest you're being right now. I appreciate it too."

"Scout has told me a bit about him," Miller says. "Sounds like he was a great guy."

Dad looks over at me, likely because he knows how big of a deal it is that I've talked about Pops with anyone, let alone with Miller. "He was the best. He loved hockey and even got me into it. He followed you in the AHL, thought you had some great potential. It's a bummer he didn't get to see the team lift the Cup."

Miller sits up straighter on the bench, his grip on my thigh growing firmer as if he's struggling with the same emotions that are coursing through me as I listen to my father talk about his husband.

"The next time we do it, it'll be for him. I promise you that."

His words are like a hug to my heart, because I know no matter what happens between us, he means them. That's just the kind of guy Miller is.

"Thank you," Dad says softly, his voice thick with emotion. He clears his throat, taking another sip of his coffee. "Your sister told me you've been writing."

I groan. "Ugh. Stevie needs to mind her own business."

A laugh rumbles out of him. "She's just excited. It's been so long since…"

I nod. "I know, but still...I don't want to rush into anything."

He tightens his lips like he has a lot more to say on the subject but decides not to.

"I'd love to read what you're writing," Miller says, and every ounce of my body tenses.

I'm already pretty particular about who I let read my work, but the thought of having Miller see has my body breaking out in a sweat.

He's looking at me so hopefully and supportively that I don't want to break his heart.

"Maybe sometime."

This elicits another surprised look from my father.

I ignore it.

We chat for a while longer about the upcoming hockey season, and my dad tells Miller what he thinks the team needs to do, and how Miller might consider trying a fake shot next time to get it past the Arizona goalie since I guess he bites on those often. Miller's nice enough to just nod and play along like he's actually going to take anything he says seriously.

When there's a natural lull in the conversation, my dad sighs and smacks the table with both hands. That's his signature move when it's time to leave.

"Well," he says, right on cue, rising from the bench, "I guess I better get out of your hair, let you get back to the truck and, you, Miller, back to hockey where I'd best see you try some fake-outs."

Miller laughs, pushing up to his feet. "Yes, sir."

This time when he extends his hand, my father shakes it.

Then my dad looks at me, opening his arms, and I fall right into them like I always do. It's a warm hug, the kind that feels like home.

"I like him," my father whispers in my ear. "And Pops would too."

Tears spring to my eyes, and I have to blink them away quickly before Miller sees them. No reason I need to embarrass myself right now.

"Thanks," I mutter, sniffling as I pull back.

He pecks a kiss on my forehead, gives Miller one last wave, then takes off.

"Well," Miller says after a few moments of silence, "I didn't realize I was meeting the family today."

I laugh. "I didn't either. He just showed up."

He lifts his hand, squeezing the back of his neck. "I, uh, noticed you kind of hesitated when introducing me."

I grimace. "You caught that, huh?" He nods. "I wasn't sure what we're labeling this or *if* we're labeling this."

"I mean, we've been seeing one another for nearly two months now. I'm okay with a label if you are."

"Really?"

"Really."

"And it's...exclusive?"

A dark look crosses his features. "I don't fucking share, Scout."

The deep rumble that leaves him almost scares me because I am not expecting the turn his mood has taken.

But oddly, I find it incredibly hot that he's being so protective over me—not that he has a reason to be. I haven't been with anyone in years, and there are absolutely zero other people I'm interested in.

"I don't want to share either."

The tension releases from his shoulders, and he relaxes. "Good."

"Good." I nod. "I guess that makes us..."

"Boyfriend and girlfriend. Another first for me," he mutters.

"I feel special I'm getting all your firsts."

He blushes at that, and it's cute to see a massive, grown-ass hockey player blush.

"So, uh, no offense or anything, but what are you doing here?"

"Right. That." He tucks his hands into his pockets and shrugs. "I'm leaving tonight, so I figured I'd pop in and see you. You know, in case you miss me while I'm gone."

"I think you'll be the one missing me."

He furrows his brows. "Of course I will."

"I am very missable."

He laughs, reaching out and grabbing one of the straps on my overalls, tugging me closer to him. He rests his ass at the end of the picnic table, and I step between his legs. It feels natural, like we've done this dance a thousand times before.

I'm not sure how to feel about it, but I do know I'm not willing to decipher it right now either.

"Come on, Girlfriend Scout, admit that you're going to miss me."

I can't help but grin at my new name.

"Your orgasms, maybe. But you?" I shrug. "Eh."

"Eh? *Eh?*" He nuzzles his nose against my cheek. "I'll show you *eh*."

He attacks me with his mouth, kissing me breathless before wrenching his lips from mine and peppering kisses along my jawline, down my neck on both sides, then back to my lips. I'm unsurprised when I'm gasping for air and basically rubbing myself against him by the time he pulls away.

"Are you sure you're not going to miss me?" he asks, a wicked grin on his face.

"I'm sure."

He captures my mouth in another heated kiss, his hands moving lower and lower until he's cupping my ass, pulling me so close I can feel his hardened cock straining against his jeans. We should stop. This is my place of business. It's entirely inappropriate what we're doing. As much as I don't want to stop—and I really don't want to —I drag my mouth from his.

"What about now?" he asks, just as out of breath as I am.

"If I say yes, will you promise to stop kissing me like that? We're going to make a scene."

"Yes."

"Then yes, Boyfriend Miller, I'll miss you."

"I don't know, I feel like you're just saying it to say it now."

"Miller…" I growl, and he laughs.

"Fine, fine. I believe you."

"Good. Because I will, Grady. I'll miss you."

It's true. He's going to be gone for a week, and I will miss him, not just because of the orgasms or the kisses, but because I like being around him entirely too much.

"Say it again."

"I'll miss you."

"No, the other part."

"Your name?" He nods. "I'll miss you, Grady."

He sighs.

And then he breaks his promise and kisses me senseless all over again.

CHAPTER 17

Miller: How's my girlfriend doing?

Scout: Wow. You're really leaning into this, huh?

Miller: Of course I am. It's a first for me.

Scout: I still can't believe that.

Miller: Well, it's true. Sadly.

Scout: But you're you. It makes no sense.

. . .

Miller: Believe it or not, I used to be shy.

Scout: Not. I definitely do not believe that.

Scout: I honestly cannot fathom it.

Miller: It's true. I didn't really start coming out of my shell until I hit the NHL. It was the first time I didn't have to be under my parents' constant watch and control.

Scout: I suppose that checks out.

Scout: It's still hard to believe you weren't always a relentless flirt.

Miller: Relentless is a good word for it. Wore you down, that's for sure.

Scout: Ugh. Don't remind me.

. . .

Miller: That you're my girlfriend?

Miller: Because you're my girlfriend, Scout.

Scout: You're loving that word, huh?

Miller: So much.

Scout: I'm glad. Now, leave me alone so I can work, boyfriend.

Miller: Sure thing…girlfriend.

Scout: You're exhausting.

Miller: I can exhaust you.

Scout: You already do.

Miller: Wait.

• • •

Miller: That wasn't a compliment, was it?

Scout: *zips lips*

Miller: Whatever. I'm taking it as one.

Scout: Shocker.

Miller: I could really go for one of your vanilla cold brew coffees this morning.

Scout: You know that's not a specialty drink only the truck has, right? You can order it pretty much anywhere.

Miller: Yeah, but it's not the same.

Miller: Plus, I'd feel like I'm cheating on you or something.

• • •

Miller: And I am NOT cheating on you, by the way.

Miller: Not with donuts or coffee or sex.

Miller: Not that we've had sex yet, but still.

Miller: NO CHEATING.

Scout: Miller?

Miller: Yeah?

Scout: Shut up.

Miller: That's fair.

Miller: Kind of got myself worked up there, huh?

Scout: Maybe a little.

. . .

Scout: But I'm happy to know you're not cheating on me.

Scout: Donuts or otherwise.

Miller: I never would. Some of these guys...the shit they do...I hate it. I don't ever want to be that person. Not like your ex.

Scout: Trust me, you're nothing like him.

Miller: Because my dick is totally bigger, right?

Scout: JESUS

Miller: It's Miller.

Scout: You can't just send me random texts like that!

Miller: What? Is it not true?

. . .

Scout: You're fishing.

Miller: I am. Are you going to take the bait?

Scout: Nah.

Miller: I'll just assume it is then.

Scout: Anyone tell you you're exhausting yet today?

Miller: Just Greer. And Smith. Then Rhodes and Wright. Lowell's the only one who has been nice.

Scout: He has a baby at home. Nothing annoys him anymore.

Miller: Fair assessment.

Miller: Shit. Coach is calling. Video-chat later?

. . .

Scout: I'm still not having phone sex with you, Miller.

Miller: BOO!

Scout: Hey, Miller?

Scout: Your dick is bigger.

Miller: I FUCKING KNEW IT!

Miller: I miss you.

Scout: I miss you too.

Scout: You totally screenshot that, didn't you?

Miller: 100%

. . .

Miller: I can't wait to see you tomorrow.

Scout: I can't either. Good night, Miller.

Miller: Good night, girlfriend.

CHAPTER 18

We have five minutes left on the clock, and we're one goal down.

I want so damn badly to beat New York right now, especially since they were the assholes to knock us out of the first round last year. We got swept, and I want to get back at them for it.

"Come on, Lowell! Fucking move!" Rhodes yells, and I guess he's feeling the same way I am. "We got this," he says, though I'm not sure if he's talking to me or himself. "I can feel it."

I fucking hope he's right. I'm not too eager for bonus hockey tonight. Tonight, all I want to do is get home and see the one person I've been dying to see for days —Scout.

Our road schedule is grueling, and we've been gone for over a week now. We've been texting and have video-chatted a few times, but it's not the same. I want to see her. I want to touch her. I just want to be around her because I really, really fucking miss her.

"Heads in the game, boys," Coach says from behind us, almost like he knows I'm not thinking about hockey right now. "We got this. We fucking got this."

We watch for cues, and as soon as Lowell comes off the ice, I hop on.

Once I'm where I need to be, off comes Greer for the extra skater. Fitzgerald barrels into the zone, looking for a wide-open spot on the left. I zing the puck over to him, and he sends it out to Wright, who zips it back to me.

I wind up and shoot.

The goalie blocks it, but the puck is still in play, and the juicy rebound goes directly for the rookie.

And, thanks to him, we score.

We skate along the bench bumping gloves but head back for the grind because the game isn't over yet. Back to center ice we go.

They blow the whistle, and the puck is dropped.

I battle with the captain of New York. He's tough... but I'm better. I get the puck loose and to Rhodes, who sends it to Wright. Off goes Greer yet again as they get the play set up. Back and forth and back, making the other team dizzy with their efforts.

Rhodes. Wright. Rhodes. Me. Rhodes.

Then right in the back of the net with just enough time to spare.

"Fuck yes!" I yell, jumping against the glass as my teammates crowd around me and celebrate.

We're back in this, and with any luck, we can score again. It's not over yet. There's still some time left on the clock, and everyone knows every single second and inch counts in hockey, so we can't get too cocky.

New York takes their timeout, and we hustle over to the bench, listening as the coaches go over everything we need to do to get the job done.

When that buzzer sounds thirty seconds later, it's my favorite victory of the season so far.

After celebrations in the locker room, we go straight to the tarmac. It's late, and we have a flight to catch because we're finally going home.

Scout's definitely asleep, so there's no way I'm seeing her tonight, but just the thought of being able to walk up to the truck tomorrow and see her smiling face has me downright giddy.

"What the hell do you look so cheery for? It's late as shit, man."

I glance over to find a rather sourpuss-looking Greer sliding into the seat next to me. "Dude, how can you be grumpy? We just won."

"I'm not grumpy. This is just my face."

I laugh because he's not exactly wrong. He does look grumpy all the time, even when I know that's not the case. "You should probably get that fixed."

He flips me off and pulls his headphones out of their case. "I plan to—with beauty rest."

"You're going to need a lot."

Another middle finger is sent my way. "Seriously, though, aside from the win, why are you so damn happy?"

"I'm excited to get home, is all."

His eyes light up at that. "That's right—donut girl. How's that going? Have you..." He looks around, then leans in close. "Did you finally ditch the v-card?"

"I'm not discussing my sex life with you."

He scoffs, looking disappointed. "That means no."

"We haven't. *Yet.*"

"Ha!" he says loudly. "I knew it!"

"Dude, shut the fuck up," I hiss, glancing around to make sure nobody is paying attention.

Most of the guys are already asleep, and a few of them are on their phones, probably with their wives. I can see Lowell's screen from here, and he's just watching his baby sleep. None of them are paying us any mind, thank fuck.

His brows slam together. "Seriously, dude? You've been hanging out with her constantly, and you still haven't hit that?"

Annoyance builds in my chest at the way he's talking about Scout like she's just a random conquest and not someone I genuinely care about.

"It's... Well, she's Scout."

"Yeah, I know who she is, numbnuts, but come on. You can't tell me you haven't had the chance—you're just too chickenshit to actually do it."

Have there been moments when I thought we'd tear each other's clothes off? Sure. Do I want to do just that every time I see her? Yes, but I really don't want her to think the only reason I'm with her is to lose my virginity, because it's not that at all.

She means so much more to me than that.

Don't get me wrong, fooling around with her is incredible, but it's not even about that.

I like her sense of humor and the way her mind works. I like how hard she works and how she gives her business her all. I like the way she treats people and how she wears her heart on her sleeve. I like her laugh and her smile, and I fucking love her body.

I just like *her*.

When I'm away from her, I miss her, and when I'm with her, the world just seems to click into place. I've never had that before. I've never found a person I want to spend all of my time with.

Scout is more than sex. She's more than just some random person I'm spending time with.

She's… "Everything."

"What?"

I gulp, then shake my head. "Nothing. It's nothing."

He looks like he doesn't believe me, like he wants to ask a million questions, but thankfully, he doesn't.

"I'm done talking to you about this."

He shakes his head. "Whatever, man. But don't come crying to me when you're turning twenty-five and still carrying that card around."

He pulls his headphones over his head, leans back against the seat, and closes his eyes. He's going to sleep.

He's going to sleep, and I'm sitting here realizing

Scout means more to me than anyone ever has before and…I think I might be in love with her.

I'm no longer sure I can wait until tomorrow to see her. It needs to be tonight.

I *have* to see her.

Our flight home is a short one, and we're landing back in North Carolina before I know it. I say my goodnights to the guys, then race to my Porsche. I don't think about the time or the implication of showing up at her apartment at this hour—I just go straight there.

The lot is fairly dark when I arrive, and I try to guess which apartment is hers from the outside of the building. There are a few with their TVs still on, and I pray one of them is hers.

I take the stairs two at a time, completely focused on getting to her door when I crash directly into someone.

"Oh shit. I'm sorry. I—Miller?"

I look up to find Scout standing in the middle of the walkway.

"Scout…what are you doing?"

"I could ask you the same thing."

"I…" I glance down at the bag she's holding in her hand. "Are you going somewhere?"

"Your place."

"My place?"

She nods, a blush stealing over her cheeks. "I wanted to see you. I was hoping you'd take pity on me and let me in for the night."

Something I've never felt before swells inside my

chest at her confession, and it's so strong I physically rub at the spot where I feel it.

She missed me too.

"What's in your bag?" I ask, taking a step closer to her.

"Clothes for tomorrow, some pajamas…"

Another step. "Pajamas, huh?"

She nods, looking sheepish.

One last step and I'm standing just in front of her, peering down at her as she looks up at me with wide, excited eyes.

I grip her chin between my fingers. "What'd I say about pajamas?"

Then I claim her mouth with mine and show her just how much I missed her.

The elevator ride up to my apartment is quiet. We're literally standing on opposite sides of the space. It's like we know if we stand too close, there's no way we're making it to my floor with all our clothes on.

And I'm really looking forward to not having my clothes on with her.

The car arrives on my floor, and we hurry down the hall to my apartment. The second we're inside, my mouth is on hers. Her back meets the door with a loud moan as I slide my tongue between her lips, tasting her for the first time in what feels like years.

I missed this.

I missed *her*.

My hand comes up around her throat, gripping her gently and holding her there as I have my way with her mouth.

"God, you taste good," I tell her, nipping my way across her jaw to that spot just below her ear. She moans when I bite down, then lick away the pain.

"Miller…" she pants.

She shoves at my suit jacket, and I shrug it down my shoulders, letting it fall to the floor in a heap. She begins plucking the buttons on my dress shirt free as my hands find the stupidly sexy yoga pants she's wearing and push them down.

She steps out of them, then yanks her shirt over her head, leaving her leaning against the door in nothing but her bra and panties. As hot as she looks right now, I want them both gone. I want her bare and spread out before me.

As if she's thinking the same thing, she pushes off the door and kisses me, trailing her mouth from mine and down my chin, over my throat, across my chest. Her descent doesn't stop as she drags her soft lips lower and lower until she's on her knees, her hands on my belt buckle.

It's a beautiful fucking sight, one I could get really used to.

But right now, it's not what I want.

I want *her*.

I've been close to this moment before, but never in my life has it felt as right as it feels tonight, as right as *she* feels.

I grab her by the chin, tugging her back, and she stands.

"Is everything okay?" she asks, worrying her bottom lip between her teeth. I ease her concern with a soft kiss, wrapping my arms around her waist.

"As much as I love the way you look on your knees for me, Scout, I was kind of thinking of something else..."

"What..." It takes a moment for what I'm asking of her to register, and when it does, she looks shocked. "Oh. Are you...sure?"

"I've never been surer of anything in my entire life."

"Okay, then."

"Yeah?" She nods. "Good."

I haul her into my arms, and her legs go around my waist on instinct. I crash my mouth to hers and carry her through the apartment and down the hall to my bedroom. I don't stop until my knees hit the bed. Then, slowly, I set her down.

I reach around and unhook her bra as I continue to kiss her, and she finally gets the buckle of my pants undone. I toss the garment somewhere off to the side as I drop to my knees before her.

She leans back on her hands as I shoulder my way between her thighs, placing soft kisses up them just as she taught me before. I kiss and lick my way to her sweet,

sweet center, treasuring the groan that leaves her when my tongue finally lands right where she wants it.

"Fuck, you taste so good," I mutter against her. "I swear I could spend an hour with my tongue on your cunt."

"I swear I'd let you," she says, shivering as I suck her clit into my mouth.

Her fingers slide through my hair, holding me to her until her legs are quaking around me and she's chanting my name.

"Grady, Grady, Grady."

She says it over and over as she comes on my tongue. When her shaking subsides, I shove up to my feet, and her hands are on my belt in an instant. She pulls my pants and boxer briefs down my thighs, and the minute my cock springs free, she wraps her lips around it, tasting me for the first time like she can't wait another second for it.

I groan, crashing my hands through her hair as she continues to lick and suck on me. I want to come. I want to bury my cock in the back of her throat and fuck her hard until she's gagging around me.

But more than that, I want to feel her come apart around my dick.

With a gentle tug at her hair, I pull her off. She peers up at me, eyes glassy and lips swollen from my kisses and her own.

"As much as I want to come down your throat, I want to come inside you even more."

Her eyes flare, and she nods, scooting back farther on the bed. I step out of my pants, kicking them away, then head for the bedside table.

I pull open the drawer and grab a condom.

She arches a brow, and I shrug.

"Wishful thinking."

She laughs, but it's cut off when I kiss her deeply. Not moving my lips from hers, I crawl onto the bed, positioning myself between her legs. I break our kiss, and with shaking fingers, I tear open the condom packet.

Scout doesn't miss it. Her hands cover mine, and I look down at her.

"Let me," she says softly, and I nod.

She pulls the condom from the wrapper, then fits it over my cock, rolling it down and giving me a few extra strokes.

"Are you nervous?" she asks, her hand still on my dick.

I shake my head. "No. I'm shaking because if you keep touching me, I'm going to come, and this will be over before it even started."

She laughs, giving me one last languid stroke before trailing her hands up my abs, tugging me down on top of her as she falls to the mattress.

I'm not lying to her; I'm not nervous. I feel like I should be, but I can't find it in me, and that's because this moment? Right here with Scout?

It's *right*.

I slide my hand between us and line my cock up with

her body.

Then, inch by delicious fucking inch, I push inside her.

"Oh god," I groan into her shoulder as I slowly slide in until there's nothing more I can give. I'm holding on to her so tightly there's no way she's not going to bruise, but I need the stability to keep me grounded because I swear it feels like I'm two seconds away from floating on air with the pure euphoria I feel right now.

"It's… You're… *Fuck.*"

She chuckles, which makes her squeeze my cock even harder, and I want to die.

Wait—no. I definitely want to keep living in this moment. In fact, I want to live like this forever, buried inside of Scout, never to return.

She feels incredible. She feels right. She feels like everything I've been missing in my life.

She feels like *mine*.

I don't want to move. I'm too scared that if I move, I'll blow my load, and this will be the most disappointing few minutes of her life.

Think of anything else, Miller. Losing in the Finals. Taking a stick to the face. Catching a puck on my boot.

"Grady…I need you to move. Please," she begs on a whisper.

And I can't deny her.

Unhurriedly, I rock my hips. It feels good, so goddamn good I can't hold back any longer. I pick up my pace, driving into her over and over, letting the sounds of her moans fill my ears as she angles her hips to meet my thrusts.

I'm literally shaking. Can feel sweat rolling down my back. I'm so damn close that if she doesn't come in the next few seconds, this is over.

I don't want it to be over.

I reach between us, letting my thumb brush over her clit, and with a few more thrusts, she's crying out.

"Oh god, oh god, oh god."

The minute her pussy squeezes my cock, I'm done for.

I come so hard I swear the life force slowly drains out of me. I collapse against her like an asshole, but I can't move.

I can't move, can't even think straight. I'm so tired and exhausted it's taking everything I have just to breathe right now.

She must not care because she wraps her arms around me, holding me tightly to her.

"You're perfect," I mutter, and I feel her laugh.

"I'm not."

"For me, Scout. You're perfect for me, and I really want to tell you something, but I'm scared you're going to freak out."

"What is it?" she asks.

But I don't answer her. Instead, I drift off to sleep, repeating in my head three words I'm too afraid to say out loud.

I love you.

CHAPTER 19

I took Miller's virginity.

I took Miller's virginity, and he told me he loved me.

He was half asleep when he said it, but I heard it all the same.

I'm sure it was nothing, though, sure it was just an in-the-moment kind of thing because hello, I'd just taken his virginity. I'm sure he would have said it to any woman at that moment.

Besides, Miller can't love me…can he?

If he does, do I even want him to?

As I peel my eyes open, I try to bury the thoughts, tucking them away to deal with later. The sun is just barely beginning to brighten the sky, and I know I should probably get up and go help Rosie at the truck, but I can't muster the energy. I'm too exhausted from last night.

I didn't have the intention of the night ending in sex and don't think he did either, but it happened. It happened, and I'm freaking out about it like it was *my* first time having sex. I can't imagine how he's feeling.

I roll over to check on him, and my stomach drops.

The bed is empty.

Oh god.

Bile rises in my throat at the realization that he's not here.

Does Miller regret it? Does he wish he could take it back, find someone else? Someone better? Thoughts race through my head so fast and so loud I barely register the room around me.

Which is why I don't notice Miller is still here until he pulls open the bathroom door and grins down at me.

"Hey, you're up," he says, his voice still scratchy from sleep. He climbs back into his bed, scooting close but not quite touching me.

I smile at him and wait for the awkwardness to settle in, but it never comes.

"How are you feeling?"

It takes all of two seconds for us to burst into laughter.

I cover my face. "Oh god, I don't know why I said that. It sounds so stupid, but I swear that's what they say in movies after someone loses their virginity, so I thought that was what I should say."

He tugs my hands away from my face. "It's fine, and I feel fine. The same, really. But also...lighter? If that makes sense. I mean, I've been building up that moment for the last twenty-four years. It was...nice."

"Nice?"

"Incredible." He rolls until he's on top of me, fitting himself between my legs like it's the most natural place in the world for him. "Amazing. The best thing I've ever done, and that includes when I lifted the Stanley Cup over my head."

I raise my brows. "That's quite the compliment to my vagina."

"It's a great vagina. But seriously…" He places a soft kiss on the tip of my nose. "Thank you. I'm…I'm really glad it was you, Scout."

"Thank me? Thank *you*. I had not one but *two* orgasms last night."

I don't know why there's emotion building up in my throat, causing it to burn, or why my eyes begin to sting, but they do.

"Thank you for trusting me."

He grins and then gives me a soft kiss, which soon turns into more.

I should probably worry about my morning breath, but at this point, I don't care. Kissing him is just too addicting.

I feel his stiffening cock against me, pressing right between my legs, which are sore in the best kind of way, and I lift my hips to brush against it.

He groans, then pulls his mouth from mine. "As much as I'd love a repeat—and I really, really would because I think I could blow your mind for an entire five minutes this time—I have practice. You're more than welcome to stay as long as you want, though. There's no rush for you to go."

"I appreciate it, but I should probably get to the truck. Rosie is great and all, but I'm still not sure I trust her to open by herself just yet."

"You work too hard. You should stay here. Rest—you deserve it."

Resting does sound nice…

But I also want to get home and grab my laptop before heading to the truck. I have an idea for a new chapter, and I want to get it out before I forget it.

I don't tell him that, though. Instead, I say, "The public needs their donuts. Do you mind if I take a shower before I go? That rain head feels like heaven."

"Funny…I thought the same about your pussy last night." I blush at his crassness and squeeze my thighs because I like the way the word sounds rolling off his tongue. He gives me another quick peck before rolling off me. "But yeah, feel free. The shower's all yours."

I fly out of bed, entirely too excited about it. He laughs, but it fades fast.

I turn to figure out what made him so quiet.

Apparently, it's me.

I can't even find the energy to be embarrassed about being so naked in front of him as the morning light slowly begins to brighten the room. I've never felt so comfortable being naked around someone before, but I do with Miller, and it's because he's looking at me like he is right now—like he wants me, like he can't get enough.

"What's wrong?" I ask, looking down to where his eyes are fixed.

It's hard to miss what he's looking at. On each of my thighs are five tiny bruises from where he was gripping me last night.

He swallows hard, then drags his eyes to mine. "Is it weird that I find that hot?"

I shake my head because if it's weird he finds it hot, it means it's weird I find it hot.

I like the idea of Miller marking me. It makes me feel like I belong to him...and I don't entirely hate the idea of it.

Careful, Scout. You're treading in deep water.

"You know...I could just drive fast," he says, his eyes still raking over my body.

"So, like you normally drive?" I tease.

"Woman," he growls.

"Dirty talk this early?" I tsk. "You're incorrigible, Grady."

His eyes spark when I say his name, and I know it's his undoing.

"Fuck it," he says, flying off the bed.

He scoops me into his arms and drags me into the shower with him.

He gripped her tightly by the waist and slammed his mouth against hers. The kiss was rough and bruising, but Charlie didn't mind. She

liked it a little rough, especially at the hands of the hot hockey player she'd been dreaming about nonstop.

When he finally released her, her knees were knocking together they were shaking so hard.

"Take my cock out," Brady said.

Charlie was eager to oblige.

She dropped to her knees and

"Hey, Aunt Scout?"

I let out a startled gasp, and my laptop almost falls off the countertop when I jump at the sudden intrusion.

I manage to save it, but the same can't be said for the three spatulas, the toothpick decorations, *and* the bowl of sprinkles I knock onto the floor.

"Oopsie," my niece says. "Sorry."

I peek up to find Macie standing at the end of the truck, a half-eaten donut that her mother ordered ten minutes ago in her hand. There's icing on her face, and even though she just scared the shit out of me, she looks adorable.

She also looks like she wants something.

"It's okay." I close my laptop and set it aside, then start cleaning up the mess I made.

This is what I get for writing while I'm at work. I get so lost in the story that I stop paying attention to what's going on around me. This is the second time this week I've been so focused on my fictional world that I've made a mess of things.

On one hand, it's a good thing I'm so immersed in the story, but I'm definitely letting it get in the way of what I should be doing. I have to stop bringing my laptop to work with me.

I've been writing like the wind over the last few days with Miller being on the road again, and I am so, so close to having the first draft finished that I'm spending every single free second I have with my fingers on the keyboard.

Though I'm not sure I want to admit it out loud, I'm scared if I don't finish this book while things are still hot and heavy with Miller, my muse may dry up, and it'll never get done.

And I really want to get it done.

"What'd you need, sweetie?" I ask when I catch her lingering at the door.

She gives me a toothy grin. "You know how Christmas is going to be here soon?"

"It's still over a month away, but yes, I'm aware of when Christmas is."

"Now that Miller is your boyfriend, do you think he'll get me Comets tickets for Christmas?"

I sputter out a laugh, grabbing a handful of toothpick decorations and tossing them into the trash can. "You can ask him."

"Like right now?"

"Well, no. He's at work, sweetie."

"No, he's not. He's here."

"A guy could get used to a welcome like this," his deep voice rumbles.

I peer up to find Miller leaning against the entrance to the truck, smirking down at the sight of me on my knees, I'm sure.

I'd be lying if I said it didn't sound appealing to me too.

I've never really enjoyed blow jobs in the past, but something about Miller makes me want to try all the things I never used to like again just to see if he'd make them better somehow.

"Hello," I say, returning my attention to the mess, hoping like hell he doesn't see how red my cheeks are right now because I am definitely thinking about things I shouldn't be.

"Hello? That's all I get?"

"Yes."

He laughs and walks farther into the truck, the vehicle creaking under his feet. His shoes come into view before his hand does. He tucks a single finger under my chin, pulling my face up to meet his.

"That's all I get?" he repeats, his voice deep and husky, sending a shiver through me.

Like my body is moving of its own accord, I rise to stand. Without a word, Miller hauls me closer, sealing his lips over mine.

Sprinkles crunch under our shoes, and I'm acutely aware that we're standing in the middle of my truck where everyone can see us, but I don't care, not when he's holding me like he is, not when his lips feel so good against mine.

I'm getting attached to him. Dangerously so.

But I can't help it. Being with Miller feels so good, so right.

He hasn't told me he loves me again, so I'm definitely chalking that up to his sleepy brain, but I'm dying to hear him utter those words again.

And that fucking scares me.

I have no idea how long we stand locked together because when he's kissing me, it feels like time is standing still. Not until someone clears their throat do I snap back to reality.

We pull apart, and I turn toward the window to find a very amused Harper and Ryan staring at us.

"Well, I have to say, I did not expect this," Harper says.

"I don't know, they were kind of giving off vibes at the fundraiser," Ryan tells her. "It's the romantic in me—I see things like this."

"Do you, though? I'm pretty sure I was the one who had to tell you that you were in love with your own husband."

"Well, technically…"

Harper rolls her eyes at her best friend. "Technicalities, my ass."

"Are you two finished?" Miller interrupts them.

Ryan laughs. "That's rich coming from you, Mr. Attack Her Mouth."

"I didn't attack her. I kissed her, and she liked it."

All three of them look at me like they're waiting for me to confirm or deny it.

"I did like it," I tell them.

"Ha! See!" Miller says.

I glare at him. "Go away. I have customers."

"Ugh. Fine." He throws his hands in the air. "I'll go see what Macie's up to."

"She wants tickets to one of your games, in case you didn't hear that earlier."

"Tickets? Hell yeah I'll get her tickets. I'll go work it out with Stevie."

He takes off out the back of the truck, and I don't miss the Chocolate Nutty Butter donut he steals on his way through.

"Ladies," he says to the girls as he walks past them.

They eye him as he stalks away, and the minute he's out of earshot, they begin peppering me with questions.

"When did this happen?"

"Are you two dating?"

"Is Miller really a good kisser?"

"Does this mean you're going to be coming to the games now?"

"Is his dick really—"

I hold my hand up, halting that last question from Ryan.

"Okay, fine." She lifts her hands. "Too far. But..." I lift my brow in warning. "Does this mean you're going to come to games? You're a WAG now, and we cool ones have to stick together. Some of the others are just so…"

"It feels like high school all over again," Harper explains.

Ryan nods. "Yes! Like that. Except worse because they all have money and look like clones."

"It's eerie even for me," Harper says. And that really is saying something considering she makes horror-themed stuff for a living. Eerie is her specialty.

"I'm assuming a WAG has something to do with dating?"

Harper nods. "Wives and girlfriends."

"Ah, gotcha."

"If you decide to come, great. You're definitely welcome. And if not, that's okay too. We know hockey games aren't everyone's scene. Hell, I didn't even like the sport until I met Collin."

"And now you're reciting stats in your sleep."

"Oh my god, Ryan, that was one time!" Harper says. "Besides, you've done your makeup witchcraft and turned yourself into how many hockey mascots now?"

"Mind your business." Ryan sticks her tongue out.

I laugh.

Maybe I should go to a game with them. I'm not sure a hockey game is really my scene, but it could be fun, and if nothing else, it'll be good book research.

Not tonight, though. Tonight, all I want to do is go home and write, especially since Macie interrupted me just when it was getting good.

"I won't be able to make the game tonight, but maybe the next one?"

Harper claps her hands together. "Yay!"

She gives me the details, and we make plans to meet up at her house so we can all drive over together for their next home game in two days.

With a promise to text them, I hand them their usual orders, and they say their goodbyes, making sure to scold Miller on their way out for not telling them about us.

"They're kind of scary sometimes," Miller says, coming back to the truck and leaning against the counter.

I laugh. "I think they're sweet."

"Did you guys make plans for a game?" I eye him. "What?" He shrugs. "I wasn't listening in the whole time."

"Just most of it."

He has the decency to at least look embarrassed. "I won't lie, I'm excited as fuck to see you at my game. You're going to wear my jersey, right?"

"You mean the one you tried to literally rip off my body, but all you ended up doing was giving me a burn?"

"I said I was sorry! *And* I kissed it better. Besides, it's not my fault they make it look so easy to rip off someone's clothes in movies."

I shake my head. "Has anyone told you lately that you're exhausting?"

"You did just last night."

I blush, thinking about what happened after he got

back from being away. They won five to nothing, and a celebration was definitely in order after a shutout.

I tried to tell him it should have been me rewarding him for such an amazing night, but he insisted me sitting on his face was his reward. I wasn't about to complain about that.

"Are we still on for our date tomorrow?"

"Yes, sir. Six?"

"Oh, say that again."

I crinkle my nose. "Six?"

"No. The *sir* part."

"I am not calling you *sir*."

"Hmm…I don't know. I'm liking the way it sounds."

"Miller…" I groan. "Go away before I do something ludicrous like listen to you."

He laughs. "All right, fine. I'm going." He leans across the counter, pressing a kiss to my cheek before walking away backward. "I'll see you tomorrow?"

"Yes, sir," I tease.

He pauses, tipping his head to the side, just staring at me with those liquid gold eyes of his.

There's something in them I haven't seen before, something I can't quite place my finger on. Whatever it is, it makes me tingle from my toes to my fingertips, and not even in a sexy way.

It's something else.

Something different.

Something good.

"What is it?" I ask him, unable to take it any longer.

"It's…" He shakes his head softly like he's rousing himself from a dream. "It's nothing."

"You sure?"

"Yep. See you tomorrow!" he calls over his shoulder as he spins on his heel and practically jogs to the parking lot.

What the hell just happened?

CHAPTER 20

I've come to a definitive conclusion: I am in love with Scout Thomas.

At first, I thought maybe my feelings for her were just clouded by a haze of incredible sex, and perhaps I was getting ahead of myself, but that's not the case at all.

Not by a long shot.

Yesterday when we were at the truck saying goodbye, I just looked at her and knew I wasn't going crazy, knew I wasn't jumping too far ahead. Sure, I've only really known her since this summer, but that's just it—I *know* Scout. And she knows me.

I know that I'm in love with her.

And I plan to tell her tonight...if I can figure out how.

Which is precisely why I'm standing outside her door, trying to convince myself to knock. I haven't ever felt this damn nervous in my life. Hell, not even the Stanley Cup Final was this nerve-wracking.

Blowing out a steadying breath, I rap my knuckles against the door and wait.

Roughly four seconds later, the door creaks open, and Scout's face fills the gap.

"You made it!" she says as she pulls the door open all the way. "You're early too."

"Yeah, we got done with videos early, so I figured I'd just head this way. I…" My words trail off as I get a look at what she's wearing.

Her hair is wrapped in a towel, and she's wearing a pair of shorts and a sports bra.

"Woman…" I growl, rushing into the apartment and closing the door behind me. "What the hell are you doing opening the door like that?"

She rolls her eyes, pulling the towel off her head and wringing her hair out into it. "Relax. People wear these things to the gym all the time."

Well, she has me there, but I still don't like it.

"I told you!" Stevie calls.

"Yes, and I ignored you," Scout yells at her sister. She turns back to me with a grin. "Hi." She kisses my cheek. "I'm so glad you're here."

"I'm glad I'm here too."

"Come on, I'll show you around."

"Hey, Grady," Stevie says from the island in the kitchen as we make our way farther into the apartment. "Please ignore the mess. People live here."

I laugh. "It's fine. I don't mind one bit." I hand over

the bouquet of flowers I'm holding. "These are for you ladies."

"Shut up!" she says, taking them from me. "This is really sweet of you. I'll grab a vase. I hope I don't kill them before dinner with Dad, because they'd make a great centerpiece."

I make a mental note to buy another bouquet for the dinner I've been invited to next week just in case.

Stevie hops down off the stool and retrieves a vase from a cabinet, getting to work arranging them.

I peek around the apartment that I'm pretty sure could fit into my living room and kitchen. The building it's in is older, but the apartment looks newly renovated with sleek hardwood floors and granite countertops. It's nice.

Stevie isn't lying—people do live in it, and that's obvious from all the knickknacks lying around and the backpack slung across the floor. It looks like a home, unlike my apartment, which sometimes feels like a museum. I don't spend much time there, especially during the season, so it's hard to even get it messy, but still. I much prefer this cozy space to the one I have.

With my schedule and Scout's, it's always easier to spend time at my apartment than here so we don't disturb Stevie or Macie. This is the first time everything worked out where we can be at her place, and I already don't want to leave.

It's just a bonus that tonight is the famous mac and cheese night I've heard so much about.

"Dinner smells great," I tell Macie, who is standing on a small stepstool at the stove, stirring the noodles. "What's the secret ingredient today?"

"It's hot dogs *and* baked beans!"

I want to curl my lips up, but at the last second, I remember I'm talking to a nine-year-old who sounds more excited than I've ever been about anything before, so I force a smile.

"It sounds…great."

"It actually is," Scout says quietly from beside me. "At first, I had the same thought you're having right now, but it was actually way better than I thought it would be."

"Guess you're getting another of my firsts," I say to her, winking.

She giggles, then grabs my hand. "Let me show you my room while I finish getting dressed."

I follow her through the apartment, and the minute she tugs me into her room and slams the door shut behind her, I'm on her. I cage her in from behind, pressing up against the door. I slip my hand around her throat, arching her head back as my lips find her earlobe. I bite down, and she lets out a gasp.

"You look fucking edible," I tell her quietly. A moan slips free when I nibble my way from that spot below her ear she loves to her shoulder. "You're killing me in this."

There's no way she doesn't *feel* that I mean it. My cock is straining so fucking hard against my jeans, and I have half a mind to rip this skimpy outfit from her body and fuck her until she's screaming my name just for being a little tease.

But I can't. We're not alone.

Instead, I do a little teasing of my own, slipping my hand around her and cupping her through the skintight cotton shorts, pressing my thumb against her clit.

"What I wouldn't give to taste this pretty cunt of yours right now…"

"Grady…" she whines. "Please."

The single word has me spinning her around and dropping to my knees in front of her, tugging her shorts down along the way. I don't waste a single second, shoving my tongue between her legs for a quick taste.

Fuck, she's sweet. The greatest thing I've ever had. I could do this forever. Could spend an eternity tasting her and making her scream.

But right now, as badly as I want to, I can't.

I pull away, tugging her shorts back up and pressing a quick kiss to her lips before putting two feet of distance between us.

It takes her a second to realize what's happening—or more accurately, what isn't happening.

When she peels her eyes open, there's no mistaking the fire in her eyes. She's annoyed she's been played.

"You're the worst," she seethes.

"What'd I do?"

She glowers, brushing past me and marching to her closet. She yanks a shirt off the hanger and puts it on angrily.

I laugh the whole time as she stomps out of her room and back toward the bathroom, all while pushing my hard cock down because she's not the only one who wishes we were alone right now.

I take a real look at her bedroom for the first time and, right away, I notice there are books everywhere. They're on the shelves that line the walls, and there are literal stacks of them on the floor. It's already a small space, so all the books in here make it feel even smaller, but it doesn't matter because it just screams Scout.

I love it. I love *her*.

I continue my perusal. There are a few pictures on the wall. Two older men—one I recognize as her dad and the other I assume is Pops—are in one photo with their arms slung around her. She's wearing a cap and gown; it must be her graduation. There are several of her and Macie and Stevie, plus a few of her with people I don't recognize but am going to assume are authors based on the backgrounds.

I scan the spines of the many books that fill the shelves. Most of them sound like romance titles, but a few are something entirely different, making me wonder if they're hers too or someone else's.

When I accidentally bump into the small writing desk in the corner, her open laptop comes to life, and a Word document is pulled up on the screen.

I shouldn't look.

I know that.

But I can't help the few words that catch my eye.

Hockey.

Virgin.

What the hell…

I lay my fingers on the mouse and scroll.

There are at least a hundred and fifty pages, and so many familiar things stick out to me as I fly through the document to get to the beginning.

Once I do, I freeze.

Pucked by the Virgin [Working Title] by Scout Thomas

I begin to read, and as the pages go on, there's one thing that's abundantly clear: This book is about us.

"What the hell are you doing?"

I jump, slamming the laptop shut and spinning around to find a very angry Scout standing in the doorway. She flies into the room and right past me, scooping up her computer and hugging it close to her chest.

"This is private, Miller! You had no right!" Her cheeks are red, and her eyes are glowing with rage.

Something I find very funny considering what I was just reading on her laptop. It sounded like a fanfiction about her scoring with the virgin of an NHL team.

Only it's not a fanfiction because it happened.

What the hell is happening?

"I'm sorry, but *I* had no right?" I ask, pointing to myself. "You wrote a fucking book about me, Scout. About *us*."

"It's not about us."

"Really? Because it sure as shit looked like it to me."

"Who cares if it is?" She laughs derisively. "This whole thing was just an experiment for you anyway. You wanted to lose your virginity, so you picked the easy target, the girl who was crushing on you and wouldn't turn you down. This isn't going to last, and you know it."

My jaw slackens, and everything inside of me aches to the bone. "Is…is that what you think about us?"

She tips her chin up but doesn't say anything.

The longer we stand here, the angrier I become.

"Has this all just been a game to you? Has everything we've been doing over the last few months just been research for your book? Using me? Like my fucking *parents* did?"

There's a flash of hurt in her eyes at my accusations, but she still doesn't say anything.

My chest feels like there's an elephant standing on it, and I can't seem to catch my breath.

I opened up to her as I'd never done before. I told her things nobody else knows about me…about my family.

I thought this was going to last.

There's a knock on the door that drags our attention.

"Uh, hey," Stevie says, pushing it open. "We can hear you, FYI."

She looks between us, then stares at Scout for a long, long time. I've seen that look before from my parents— it's disappointment.

With one last glance my way, Stevie pulls the door shut.

I look back over at Scout, but she's not looking at me.

She's staring down at the computer tucked tightly to her chest.

I don't like it. I don't like that she's not seeing how fucking hurt I am right now because I'm really hurt. This wasn't what I was expecting from her. I know she's been guarded with me, know she's been hurt in the past, but this? This isn't what I thought would come of this.

I step toward her, and only then does she finally look up.

"I have news for you, Scout." Her hazel eyes meet mine as she bites down on her bottom lip. "This wasn't a game to me. This wasn't about losing my virginity. This was real for me. I trusted you. I fell for you." I swallow hard, cupping the back of my neck and squeezing because that damn tension is back. "I fucking *fell for you*. I...I love you, but all I am to you is a plot point."

Her jaw drops, but nothing comes out.

She doesn't refute my words. She doesn't tell me I'm wrong. She just stands there in silence, and I swear it hurts worse than taking one of Wright's slapshots to the boot.

I have no clue how long we stand there, how long she stares at me wide-eyed, how long she keeps not saying a word...

But it's long enough for me to know one thing—I'm right, and I've never hated it more.

CHAPTER 21

SCOUT

I've somehow managed to piss off everyone in my life that I care about in the last week.

Macie? According to her, I ruined the magic of mac and cheese night.

Stevie? She's giving me the silent treatment because she heard the entire thing.

Rosie? I snapped at her this morning and sent her home for the day, then closed the truck early.

And Miller? Well, that one is obvious.

He told me he loves me, and I stood there. I was frozen, completely taken aback.

Sure, he's said it to me before, but that time he was in a post-sex sleep haze. It didn't mean anything.

This time, he was wide awake and not freshly fucked.

And he meant every damn word.

I can't believe he found my stupid book. I snort a laugh because it's not even really a book; it's a writing exercise I've been doing, a silly fluff piece that's supposed to help get my brain moving. I've been doing an online course for creative writing, and one of the suggestions was to start a story that was pure fluff, something fun and off the cuff. I started writing about the virgin hockey player and the bookworm because it was a great trope and because it still blows my mind that he could possibly be interested in me.

But it's completely fictional. Sure, the character looks like him and plays hockey and is a virgin and the heroine reads romance novels, but that's it. Nothing else in the book is about him or us or anything we've done together. It's completely made up and means nothing to me.

Miller didn't let me explain that, though. He just got upset and dropped a massive three-word bomb on me then left.

Macie cried for half an hour because she thought it was the combination of hot dogs and baked beans that made him leave. When I told her it was my fault he left and not hers, she stopped speaking to me.

Her mother followed suit soon after, which is why Stevie is now angrily cleaning the kitchen as I mope on the couch, watching *The Princess Diaries* movies over and over again because they remind me of Miller.

She slams the cabinet closed for the third time, and it grates on my nerves just a little bit more. I turn up the volume on the TV.

She slams it even louder. Then, I swear to God, she gets a pot out and begins banging it with a wooden spoon.

I've officially had enough.

"Stop!"

She bangs on the pot harder. "No!"

"Knock it off, Stevie. You're being childish!" I yell back.

"Me? *I'm* being childish?" I hear her stomp across the apartment. She doesn't stop until she's standing directly in front of the TV. She reaches behind the flat screen and yanks the cord out of the wall, her chest heaving with anger as she stands there with her hands on her hips. "You're the one acting like a mopey teenager right now, which is absolutely hilarious when you think about it because you're not the one with a broken heart."

"Then why does it feel like I am?" I scream.

The words fly out of my mouth before I even realize what I'm saying.

"Why does it feel this way?" I whisper.

I was hurt when Aaron cheated on me. Hell, it fucking broke my heart, but it felt different than this. I felt betrayed and embarrassed.

With Miller...it's anguish.

Stevie sighs heavily, then drops down onto the couch next to me. She pats my thigh. "Because you love him, you idiot."

For the first time since Miller walked out of this apartment a week ago, I cry—full-on, body-shaking, snotty crying. It's ugly and awful and makes me feel like garbage, but I deserve it because I made Miller feel the same way because I'm too freaking scared to admit I am hopelessly in love with him.

Stevie shoves tissues at me, then hands me a glass of water. She wraps a blanket around my shoulders as I gulp it down, then she takes the empty cup and sets it on the table. She sits back down next to me and pats her thighs.

I lay my head on her lap just like I used to when we were kids, and she runs her fingers through my hair in soothing strokes. I don't know how long we sit like that in the silence, but it's long enough for my shakes to subside.

"You know," Stevie says after a while, "I guess I'm just surprised. You've had a crush on him for like two years or something. How is this not what you always wanted?"

"That's just it, Stevie—it was a crush, a harmless, silly, schoolgirl crush. He's the jock. I'm the bookworm. We make no sense together. My crush was safe because it was fantasy."

"But now it's not. It's real."

"Yes." I groan, pushing off her lap and sitting up, tugging the blanket tighter around me. Maybe if I wrap myself up tightly enough, it'll act as a shield and protect me from the absolute heartache I'm feeling right now. "It's so fucking real, and I don't know if I'm ready for it to be real."

Stevie frowns, and I hate it because it's full of pity.

"You want to know what I think?"

"No."

"I think you're being stupid."

"I said I didn't want to hear it."

"Well, tough shit, because I'm going to say it. You're being stupid, Scout. This man loves you. Like *loves* you."

"Don't forget that he didn't even know who I was just earlier this summer."

"No." She points at me. "Don't do that. If you told him you forgive him, you actually need to forgive him. You're not allowed to keep bringing it back up. Besides, if you think he doesn't regret not paying attention to you for the last several years, you're sorely mistaken. The way you look at one another…" She shakes her head with a small laugh. "It reminds me of Dad and Pops."

I know she doesn't say that lightly. Our dads had a love story for the ages, meeting young and losing touch, then reconnecting years later. Their story was always one of my favorites to hear, and I'd beg Pops to tell it to me.

If Stevie is right and Miller loves me even a fraction of how much Dad and Pops loved each other, it's a hell of a lot.

"Do you love him, Scout?"

I swallow back the lump in my throat and nod. "So much. I think I fell for him the minute he walked onto the lot."

"Then tell him. However you need to do it, tell him. Don't let it pass you by. You deserve the kind of happily ever after you're always reading about, the kind you've always wanted to write."

Her words strike something inside of me, and I rise from the couch, dropping my blanket shield.

"Where are you going?" Stevie asks as I march to my

bedroom.

"To write."

She lets out a loud "Woohoo!" as I sit down at my desk and take a deep breath.

Then, I open my laptop…and I write.

"Hey, Scout, I'm taking my first ten!" Rosie calls from inside the truck.

Keeping one hand on the keyboard, I lift the other and wave so she knows I heard her.

I'm surprised I mustered even that.

For the last few days, my laptop has been attached to me, practically becoming another limb. I've barely made time to eat and sleep. It's safe to say I trust Rosie with the truck because even when I am here, I'm not truly present.

My whole life has revolved around this book. I'm addicted to the characters, to the way they make me feel. I channel it all into the story, all my heartbreaks and my pain, every single up and down I've felt over the years.

And, more than anything, I pour love into it. My love for baking, for writing.

For Miller.

Even though I've been immersed in a fictional world and have fallen in love with fictional characters, my love for him hasn't waned. If anything, it's grown stronger. I miss him so badly. Every day he doesn't show up at the truck is another day my heart aches, but I know I need this time. I need it not just to finish my book but to find the woman I lost over the last three years. It sucks to be away from Miller, but it's necessary too. I don't love who I am right now, so how can I be expected to love him the way he deserves?

"What are you writing there?"

I jump at the sudden intrusion then spin around to find my dad standing a few feet away.

"Dad!" I rise from the bench and throw my arms around his neck.

He's startled by my reaction, and I am too. It's not that I don't always love seeing my father—I do, but I don't usually react so strongly like this.

I think deep down, I've been needing him. He was understanding during the dinner Miller missed when I told him he couldn't make it because of hockey. I hated lying to him, but I didn't want to get into the real reason he wasn't joining us. I think Stevie told him anyway, but true to my father's nature, he stayed out of it until I was ready.

He must have known today was that day.

My dad squeezes me back, hugging me so tight I struggle to catch my breath. When he finally releases me, I don't even realize I'm crying until he reaches out and wipes a stray tear from my cheek.

"How's my girl doing?"

"Not good, Dad," I say on a sniffle. "I feel…rotten."

"Rotten?"

I nod. "Like from the inside out. Just...I feel all wrong. The only thing keeping me going is finishing this book."

His eyes light up at my words. "As sorry as I am that you're hurting, I'm glad you have something to help you keep pushing through."

"Me too." I sniffle again, annoyed by the way my eyes start to sting. I've cried over Miller a lot in the last few weeks, and it's no one's fault but my own.

"You, uh, want to talk about it?" Dad asks, shoving his hands into his pockets, tipping his head to the side.

"I think I'd like that." The words surprise even me. "I'll grab us some coffees."

I head for the truck, and my first stop is to grab a napkin and clean up my face from crying. I pour us two iced coffees and grab some donuts then set the *Be Right Back* sign out so Rosie can keep enjoying her break.

When I get back, Dad is not-so-subtly reading what's on my screen.

I'm not even mad, mostly because I'm proud as hell of what I'm writing. For the first time in a really long time, it feels *right*.

I set our drinks and snacks on the table, sliding in across from him. When he finally peels his eyes from the screen and looks up at me, there are tears brimming them.

"This..." He clears his throat. "This is amazing, Scout."

"You think so?"

He nods, taking a sip of his coffee. "Yes. The best you've written to date, if I do say so."

"I think so too, but you're not just saying that because you're my dad, are you?"

"Nah. If it were trash, I'd give it to you straight. We both know that."

I chuckle, because he really would.

We eat our donuts in silence for a few minutes before Dad finally asks the question I've been dreading.

"What happened with Miller?"

I set my donut down with a sigh then laugh because, without even realizing it, I picked up Miller's favorite.

"I messed up."

"*You* messed up?" Dad asks, one bushy brow raised.

"I...I closed myself off from him just when things started getting real. I told him we didn't have a future together, said it meant more to him than it did me...and when he looked me in the eyes and told me he loved me, I didn't say a word."

Dad winces. "Ouch."

"Yeah." I nod. "Ouch indeed." I groan, scrubbing my hand over my face. "Am I broken?"

"If you're broken, I'm broken too."

"What do you mean?"

Dad sighs and rests his arms on the table, leaning forward. "I mean, we're a lot more alike than you may believe. I know you and Pops always had this incredible bond, and I loved that for both of you because you and I had our things too, but what I mean this time is *this*"—he waves his hand between us—"right now, *this*...we push people away. People we care about, people we love. And we do it because we're scared of getting hurt. Hell, I did it years ago with Pops when we lost touch for all those years, and I'm doing it now because he was unfairly taken away too early, so I'm pissed about it and sulking."

"We have reasons to be cautious, though."

He nods. "You're right. We do, but at what point is that impeding on who we are as people? At what point does that become who we are? How does that shape our lives? We can't hide forever. *You* can't hide forever, Scout."

I gulp because he's right. I *can't* keep hiding. Especially not when I know now what it feels like to truly live.

And that's all because of Miller.

"How do we get better?" I ask him.

"Time. Practice. Finding the right people who will help us." He blows out a heavy breath. "That's kind of why I came here today, actually."

"Okay..." I draw the word out, not quite sure what he's getting at.

He lifts his hand and strokes his beard a few times, then says, "I met someone."

His words send so many emotions through me: shock, anger, and happiness just to name a few. I wasn't expecting him to say that, mostly because I didn't realize he was even looking for someone.

"I didn't know you were dating," I say carefully.

"I'm not. Not yet, anyway. But, uh, he asked, and…"

"You said yes."

"I said yes." He takes another drink of his coffee, and I don't miss the way his hand shakes.

He's nervous to tell me this. Why?

"I know you loved Pops, and you know I loved Pops too, so damn much that even three years later, it still hurts like we lost him just yesterday. But…I've been hiding, holed up in that house that reminds me of him, doing all the things we used to do together, which also just reminds me of him. I need something different if I'm ever going to move on. And I do need to move on." He reaches across the table, gripping my hand tightly. "It's time, Scout. For both of us."

There's a ridiculous, childish part of me that hates the idea of him moving on, that feels like he's betraying Pops by doing so. It's wrong, and I know that.

He loves Pops. He'll always love him. But he can't be alone forever, and Pops wouldn't want that either.

"I'm happy for you, Dad," I tell him, meaning every word. His face lights up at my statement, and I think he needed to hear it more than he realizes. "I think this will be really good for you."

"It can be good for you too, you know. I know losing Pops was hard, and then that little dickhead Aaron broke your heart, but we can't keep letting that hold us back. We have lives to live, adventures to have. We have people who want to be loved by us. We need to go experience all of that."

The more he talks, the more I know what he's saying is exactly what I need.

"You're right."

"Of course I'm right. I'm your dad."

He winks, and I laugh. It's a good laugh, one I really needed.

"For what it's worth, I'm happy for you too. I think this"—he dips his head toward my laptop—"will be really good for you. And so will Miller, whenever you're ready."

I blow out a steadying breath. "I think you may be right about that too."

"I am," he says confidently. He grabs his coffee and sucks down the rest of it then pushes to his feet. "I'm going to get out of here and let you get back to writing."

"You don't have to go."

What I don't say is that I *am* itching to get back to writing. I didn't write for three years, and now I have a book pouring out of me so fast I'm getting whiplash from it.

"I do. I have a date to prepare for, and you have work to do." He lifts his brows pointedly, and I have a feeling the work he's talking about isn't just my writing.

"Okay."

I stand and meet him at the end of the table, and he wraps me in one of his hugs again. This time, I don't cry.

This time, I feel refreshed.

I feel ready.

CHAPTER 22

Normally I'd head to Scout's truck after practice, but that's not really an option right now.

So here I am, walking toward Wright, Rhodes, and Lowell with a tray in my hand, hoping like hell I can use them as a distraction because I badly need one.

"So, then," Wright says as I take a seat, "his boyfriend looks at me and goes, 'Oh, you're not William.'"

All the guys laugh, but I'm completely confused as to what's going on.

"What are you guys talking about?" I ask.

"Wright's brother is in town and brought his boyfriend along with him. They're staying over at his and Harper's place," Harkens, one of our other teammates, explains. "Wright came home from practice yesterday, and the boyfriend answered the door with his lips puckered up for a kiss, thinking it was Wright's brother."

"No shit?" I chuckle. "What'd you do?"

"I kissed him," Wright answers with a shrug. "I

couldn't leave the guy hanging."

Everyone laughs again.

"Harper asked me all night long who the better kisser is, him or her."

"And?" Rhodes asks.

Wright smirks. "I told her it was a tie just to fuck with her. She hasn't talked to me all morning. I can't wait for makeup sex later."

"You're crazy, man," Harkens says, rising from his chair and clapping Wright on the back. "I'm out of here. Got to get home—my kid is potty training, and based on the text from my wife, let's just say there's a mess waiting for me when I get there."

Harkens and a few other guys take off, leaving me with just Wright, Rhodes, and Lowell.

"So, what's up with you lately, Miller?" Rhodes takes a drink of his Gatorade, eying me.

"Yeah, I feel like you haven't really been around to annoy us," Lowell says.

"I heard he has a girlfriend," Wright tells them.

"That so?" Rhodes shoots his eyes my way. "Anyone we know?"

I roll my eyes because it's clear they know about Scout and me, and I assume they heard it from their wives. I guess they missed the rest of the story, though.

"Ha, ha. You're all a bunch of comedic geniuses."

"I think we're fucking hilarious," Lowell deadpans.

I grunt, stabbing at the pasta on my plate and shoveling a bite into my mouth.

"Uh-oh. Trouble in paradise already?" Rhodes asks.

"Huh?" I look up.

He nods toward my food. "You just stabbed that pasta so hard you bent your fork."

I look down at the metal utensil in my hand, and sure enough, it's bent.

I'm not entirely surprised, though. I'm angry. So damn mad. How the fuck could Scout say we meant nothing to her and there's no future for us? How could she just stand there and stare at me when I poured my heart out to her?

It hurts really fucking bad.

"You okay, man?" Lowell asks, caution lacing his voice.

I toss my now useless silverware down with a sigh, running a hand over my face. It's been a long two weeks, and I'm tired. Every time I lie down in bed and close my eyes, all I can see is Scout standing there staring at me like I'm insane as I confess that I'm in love with her. I've been running on about four hours of sleep a night, and I'm barely eating enough to have the energy to skate.

It's not good for a lot of reasons. I need to get my shit together and fast.

"Miller?" Wright prompts when I don't say anything. There's worry laced in the single word, and fuck if it doesn't make me feel some shit I really don't want to right now. "You can talk to us, you know. About anything."

I know that. I do. It's just…I don't know if I want to

talk about this because it sucks so bad.

But they've all been here before. Maybe they'll know what I should do.

"I'm a virgin," I blurt out. Then I laugh sardonically. "Well, not anymore I'm not, but I was...until Scout. Greer knew, and the fucked-up thing is that I didn't even know I liked her until he flirted with her, and I hated it because I wanted it to be *me* flirting with her. Then one thing led to another, and now we're having sex, and it's great and not the problem at all. The problem is I'm in love with her, and I told her, and she said nothing. This was *after* I found out she's been writing a fucking book about us. I'm not even that upset about that part. I'm more pissed about the fact that I laid it all out there for her, and she just stood there, looking at me like *I'm* the asshole for having the audacity to fall in love with her. But can I really be blamed? She's amazing. She's smart and gorgeous and does this really cute thing where she mimics all the facial expressions the characters do when she's reading her books, and I just really, really love spending time with her, and it's all I want to do. I'm..." I suck in a sharp breath then exhale. "I'm hopelessly fucking in love with her and yet still so damn upset with her."

There's a hushed silence that falls over the table. I don't want to look up; I'm too scared to see the expressions on their faces.

But I'm curious too.

I sneak a glance at Rhodes and—*holy fuck*. Is he

smiling?

I look at Wright and Lowell, and they're doing the same thing.

"What?" I ask.

They all burst out laughing.

Wright grabs his water bottle off his tray and takes a big drink, shaking his head. "You're definitely in love, dude."

"I know. That's what I said."

"Yeah, but like, you're *really* in love," Rhodes tells me.

"I know," I say again.

"Like really, really in love."

"I fucking know!" I practically yell. It pulls the attention of someone walking by, and I sink lower into my seat. "I know," I repeat, this time quieter. "What do I do? What if she doesn't love me back?"

Nobody says anything for a long time, and I fucking hate it because it makes all the fears I have that much more real.

"Harper didn't love me. At least not right away," Wright confesses. "I fell for her first."

"Really?"

He nods. "Yeah. It, uh, definitely took some time for her to reciprocate those feelings. It hurt to hear at first, I won't lie. Like really fucking hurt. I'd rather take ten puck hits from Beast than ever feel that shit again."

"That's how I feel right now. Like I'm bruised and broken, and everything just feels...wrong. Is that weird?"

The guys all shake their heads.

"I'm so mad at her and love her so much at the same time. Is *that* weird?"

"No, man. It sucks, but that's love sometimes," Wright says.

"What did you do in the meantime? When it took Harper time to come around, I mean."

"I waited for her." He shrugs. "She was worth it, so I waited."

"How? How did you just wait?"

He chuckles. "Fuck, man. I'm not really sure because it honestly about killed me. But I knew I had to give her the space she needed to figure out what she wanted, how she really felt about me. Luckily, in the end, everything worked out, but…"

I gulp. "I need to figure out how to move on if she doesn't love me back."

He nods solemnly, a grimace on his face.

I hate it, absolutely loathe the possibility that he could be right, that I might just have to accept that Scout will never feel the same way for me as I feel for her.

But…I don't believe that's true. I know her. I can read her easily. There's no way this is a one-sided thing. She has feelings for me; I know it.

Maybe Wright is right. Maybe all she does need is time.

And I guess that's what I'm going to have to give her.

"Can we circle back to that virgin thing and why the fuck Greer knew about it before us?" Rhodes asks, and we all laugh, the tension dissipating.

So, I tell them everything.

"Mr. Miller?"

I turn to find one of our security guards waiting for me in the parking garage. We just got out of a game we won no thanks to me. I haven't been able to score in weeks. Can't remember the last fucking time I shot a puck and it didn't sail about three feet outside the goalie's crease.

I'm off my game. The team knows it, and Coach knows it too. It looks bad, and if I keep this shit up, I'm screwed. I can tell Coach is about one game away from dropping my ice time, and I really don't want to lose it. I might be sucking out there, but hockey is the only thing keeping me sane right now. I need the push, need the burn and the pain. I need something to keep me going because I'm really starting to feel like it's hopeless to keep waiting on Scout.

"Hey, Dom. What's up?"

"Someone dropped this off for you." He holds a huge yellow envelope my way.

I look down at it then back at him. "What is it?"

"I'm not sure." He shrugs. "I mean I opened it to make sure it wasn't dangerous, but it's just a bunch of pages with typing on them. I didn't read them all, though," he rushes out.

"Okay…" I say, taking the envelope from his outstretched palm. "Thanks," I mutter.

"No problem. Have a good night, Mr. Miller."

I stare at the heavy package the entire way to my car. Hell, I'm so preoccupied with it and what it could be, I even walk *past* my car.

When I get inside, I decide to wait to open it, tossing it onto my passenger seat and throwing the car in drive.

I make it two miles before I'm pulling off into a random lot. When I look up to see where I am, I laugh.

Of fucking course.

The dirty, ripped screen of the old drive-in taunts me…but not as much as the envelope.

I pick it up and tear it open. I know instantly what it is and who it's from, and it makes my heart ache because I miss her.

It's been almost a month since I saw her last, which is too damn long if you ask me.

Everyone's getting ready for the Christmas break. They're all fucking holly and jolly, and I've never felt more like the Grinch in my entire life. If you'd asked me last month what my Christmas plans were, I'd have said I was going to spend the holiday naked and wrapped up in Scout, but now I'm going to spend it alone, drowning in vodka and waiting.

I know I need to give her time like Wright said, but it's hard as hell to stay away. I want to march up to her truck and tell her she's wrong, tell her the thing between us wasn't something meaningless—tell her it meant *everything*.

She means everything.

I told her that, though. She knows how I feel. So now, I wait.

And waiting fucking sucks.

I stare down at the stack of pages and the sticky note on top.

Grady,

This is the book I should have written.

This is how I feel about you.

Yours,

Scout

For a minute, I simply stare at the note, because I am, admittedly, scared. I'm terrified this is going to be her way of telling me to fuck off because she doesn't feel the same as I do and she never will, her way of telling me I need to just move on and this really did mean nothing to her.

But then my eyes track down to her signature.

Yours.

Maybe...just maybe...I have a chance.

And so, I begin to read.

CHAPTER 23

The bass of the music thrums through my body, and one thing rings loud and clear in my head: Hockey games are so not my thing.

"This is amazing!" Macie shouts from beside me, headphones covering her ears because even to her, this place is too loud. "I love it so much!"

The grin on her face is contagious, and I smile down at her. "I'm glad you're having fun."

"What?" she yells.

I laugh, shaking my head.

Miller and I might not be in a good place, but he kept his word to my niece and got her tickets to his game for Christmas. I didn't let anyone see, but I cried when I saw his handwriting scrawled across the envelope that was tucked into the branches of the decorated tree. How he got the tickets to Stevie, I'm not sure, but I suppose I shouldn't be surprised. Miller has his ways.

I can't believe it's been a whole month since I've seen

him. I miss him terribly, more than I've ever missed anyone in my life, but I'm also glad I've taken time away.

I've spent the month writing, and with that have come so many emotions I wasn't prepared for. At Stevie's insistence, I sought therapy, and I learned so much about myself, like how I never really grieved the loss of my father and just buried myself in work and in fantasy to pretend I was okay.

Along with seeing a therapist, I joined a book club and made new friends.

I took up knitting. I suck at it, but it's fun.

I tried new restaurants and ate oysters. It was an awful experience, but I did it.

I *lived*.

And I feel good. Better than I ever have.

"I can't believe you actually came," Harper says beside me. "We've been asking for months and now you're finally here!"

Luckily, even with whatever Miller and I have been going through, the girls haven't stopped coming by the truck. If anything, they and their partners have been stopping by more frequently. Even Greer's been coming once a week. I'm not sure if they're doing it because of Miller, but I appreciate it either way.

"Do you love it yet?" Ryan asks.

"It's…okay."

Harper gasps dramatically, Ryan rolls her eyes at her reaction, and I laugh.

Ryan hitches her thumb toward Harper. "Can you

believe this woman used to hate hockey? Her sister too, and now she has a kid with the captain."

"She's made quite the one-eighty," I say.

"It's wild how much your life can change in such a short amount of time," Emilia chimes in with a sly grin. She definitely has the big-life-change thing down, going from a social media manager to director and dating one of the former players turned coach.

They've all had big life changes in the last few years. I've watched from the sidelines as they've gone after what they wanted.

And now…now it's my turn.

The lights dim and the music swells—if that's even possible—as the players begin to skate out onto the ice for warmups.

"Look! There's Wright!" Macie points. "And Beast! And the captain!"

She's practically standing on her seat to see everyone, though I'm not sure why. Miller hooked her up with tickets right along the glass.

Wright, Rhodes, and Lowell all skate by, banging their sticks against said glass right in front of Macie, who squeals with delight. Rhodes even launches a puck over for her when he sees she's wearing his jersey.

My eyes search the ice, looking for the guy whose number I'm wearing.

"There he is!"

Macie points across the way, and my breath is stolen from my lungs.

He has his skate up on the bench as the equipment manager fixes something, but he's not paying him any attention.

No.

He's looking at me.

The warmth of his gaze washes over me, and I swear I can feel it down to my toes. I missed it, missed the way he looks at me like I'm the only person in the room. Even in this arena filled with thousands of people, I still feel like it's just us in here.

I missed this feeling more than I've ever missed anything before.

Does he miss it too? Does he miss me? Can he forgive me? Did he read my book? I wonder if he liked it, if he realized the love story in it is ours. It's everything I feel for him and more.

I want to ask him that and so many other things, but I can't.

Not yet.

So instead, I lift my hand, and I wave.

I swear I see his lips twitch.

And it's the greatest ounce of joy I've felt in a month.

Game Two

Miller got Macie tickets to more than one game.

This time when I wave to him across the ice during warmups, he nods.

Game Three

He waved back.

And I'm slowly starting to see the appeal of hockey.

Game Four

He smiled.

He smiled, and I fucking melted.

Game Five

Macie hasn't come with me to the last two games. At this point, I'm a legit Carolina Comets fan.

I love watching the way they glide across the ice, the hits they land, the way they fight for one another, and, of course, the goals they score.

The team's on a winning streak, and the excitement surrounding it is infectious. I'm so entranced by the game that it takes a few tries of Harper tapping on my arm for me to realize someone's trying to get my attention.

"Huh?"

She points up at the big man looming at the end of the aisle.

"Scout?"

"Yes?" I ask, unsure what this is about.

The man, who has the word SECURITY on the front of his shirt, hands me a sticky note. "This is for you."

"Thank you," I mumble, taking the square paper and staring at it in wonder.

It's the same one I stuck to my manuscript, only now there are two lines written on the back.

"What is it?" Ryan asks, leaning over Harper to see what's going on.

"It's a note," Harper tells her, and I hear her add, "I think it's from Miller."

I don't join in on their speculation.

I can't. I'm too focused on the words scrawled in black ink.

Meet me after the game.
  You know where.

CHAPTER 24

MILLER

I lean against the back of my car, waiting.

We got out of the locker room thirty minutes ago, and I drove straight here. I'm hoping she's going to show and just got stuck in post-game traffic. I pick up the bottle of chocolate water and take a swig, hating how much I love it.

Ten minutes go by.

Twenty.

Thirty.

"Five more minutes," I promise myself.

But when it comes and goes, my hope begins to fade, and I decide to call it a night.

I thought maybe with her coming to my games, this might be it, thought she might be ready.

I could be wrong, and it could just be wishful thinking. Maybe that damn sticky note was a stupid idea and pushed her even farther away.

I couldn't stop myself from writing it, though.

I fucking miss her.

Seeing her at my game after Christmas, I felt hope for the first time in a long time. I felt like maybe this wasn't all in my head, like maybe she could love me too.

Then she came back.

Again and again and again.

And each time I saw her, I felt that pull I have toward her grow even stronger. I *had* to do something, even if nothing resulted from it.

It looks like that's what is happening right now.

It's been forty-five minutes.

She's not coming.

I shove off my car with a sigh and head for the driver's side door. Just as I'm popping it open, headlights swing into view, and I freeze.

Then, I hear the squeal of brakes, and I know.

She came.

Her old, beat-up Toyota rattles into the lot as she pulls up next to me. I can't see much inside the car thanks to the glare from the headlights, but I hear her door open, hear her feet hit the pavement and take quick steps toward me.

She steps in front of the light, and everything in my world feels okay again.

She's as beautiful as she's always been. Her hair is a little shorter, hitting just above her shoulders now, and somehow her hazel eyes look brighter than they ever have, but she still looks like Scout.

My Scout.

"Hello," she says quietly.

The corners of my mouth twitch. I take a step toward her.

Her breath hitches when I do, so I take another.

And another.

I don't stop until I'm mere inches away, until I can smell that all-too-familiar scent of sugary sweetness coming off her.

"That's all I get?"

That's all it takes.

I have no idea who grabs who first. All I know is our mouths are fused together, and I feel whole for the first time in over a month. Her body presses against mine, and I grip her waist, holding her closer because I'm so fucking scared she's going to disappear, and I'll wake up, and this will all have been nothing but a cruel, cruel dream.

I'm not sure when we stop kissing, but we do eventually. We don't move, though. We stand there, holding on to one another, our lips still resting against each other.

"Miller..." she says quietly. "I'm sorry."

I shake my head. "It's okay."

"It's not." She pulls her head back to look at me. "I was so dumb. I was so scared of getting hurt that I didn't let myself even try with you. You trusted me. You opened up to me. You let me in. You *gave* yourself to me, and I just pretended it was nothing. I made you feel like it didn't matter when it did—when it meant everything. And that stupid book..." She laughs. "I swear it wasn't about us. It was just a silly writing exercise. I…" She shakes her head. "I'm just so sorry."

"It's okay, Scout." I press my lips to her forehead. "It's okay."

"How can you say that, Miller? After the hurt I put you through, how can you say that?"

"Because I love you."

"You…do?"

I laugh. "Are you kidding me? Of course I do. You're…" I exhale. "You're everything, Scout. I waited so long to have something that felt good, something that made me happy and woke me up from the same shit I was doing over and over. It turns out I was waiting for you."

She peers up at me, her eyes brimming with tears. "I was there the whole time, Miller."

"I know," I tell her, running my thumb over her cheek. "I know you were. I'm so sorry I didn't before, but I see you now. I see you, Scout, and I'm never letting you go."

"Good, because I don't want you to. This time without you… I missed you."

I grin. "I knew you would."

She laughs, shoving at me playfully. "Glad to see you're still annoying."

"I'll annoy you forever if you'll let me."

She sighs, resting her head against my chest. "That sounds…nice."

"Yeah?"

"Yeah." She nods then peers up at me. "I, uh, did some soul-searching while we were apart, and forever doesn't scare me anymore. Not with you."

Fuck, her words hit me right in the chest. I needed to hear them so much more than I expected.

"I'm glad because forever with you doesn't scare me either. You weren't just an experiment, Scout. You could never be that."

"I know. I'm so sorry I said that. And the book...it was stupid. I wrote something way better."

"I know. I read it."

Her eyes widen. "You did?"

I nod. "Even the sex scenes." Red tinges her cheeks, and I laugh. "Don't be embarrassed—they were hot."

She tries to bury her face in my chest, but I don't let her.

"Don't hide. I loved it, truly. Are you going to publish it?"

She lifts her shoulders. "I'm not sure. I think I want to, but I don't know the first thing about publishing."

"I'll help you," I tell her, and I will. I don't know shit about it either, but I'll learn for her. "And if you want to submit it to agents, I'll help you with that too."

She grins. "You're really something, you know that?"

"I'm the best kind of something."

She sighs, dropping her head to my chest. "You really are."

I have no clue how long we stand there with her wrapped in my arms and me not letting her go. However long it is, I know it's not long enough, because it never could be.

"Hey, Grady?" she says after a while.

"Hmm?"

"I love you, you know."

"I knew you couldn't resist me."

"Ugh," she groans, trying to shove out of my grasp. "Shut up, Miller."

I tug her back to me, cupping her face with my hands. "Make me."

She presses her lips to mine…and she does.

EPILOGUE

I did it.

I look around the room with a wide smile, proud of everything I've managed to accomplish over the last year.

Everyone is here to celebrate with me, and I still can't believe this is my life.

"To Scout!" From beside me, Miller shoots me that grin of his that's become my favorite thing in the world. "My favorite girl, my favorite donut maker, and now my favorite published author." He winks. "I'm so proud of you, woman."

"Miller..." I groan, but even with him calling me *woman* in front of everyone, I can't seem to wipe the smile off my face.

I don't think I've ever been happier than I am at this moment.

"To Scout!" everyone echoes, lifting their glasses in the air.

I smile at them politely, dying on the inside at all the attention.

When Miller said he was throwing me a party, I laughed it off, but I should have known he wasn't kidding.

He really wasn't kidding: he rented out an entire room at a hotel that cost way too much, hired a DJ, got catering, and invited about a hundred people I don't know. It's over the top and completely ridiculous, but it's all Miller, which makes me love it.

He wraps his arm around me, pulling me in close. I slide mine around his neck the best I can.

"I mean it—I'm incredibly proud of you. You published a book *and* sold another! Can you believe it?"

"I truly can't."

That silly story I started about the virgin hockey player? After some heavy edits, Miller convinced me to keep it and self-publish it under a pseudonym. I did, then I wrote and published two more with plans for another three in the series. The sales have been steady, and the reviews are solid so far. I'm damn proud of my work.

I'm equally proud of the other book my agent sold, the one I sent to Miller. I started querying right away and somehow managed to land an agent who was okay with me wanting to be a hybrid author. A month ago, I got the news I'd been waiting for since I was a kid: my book got picked up by a publisher.

We just finalized the contract this morning.

"Nobody I know deserves this more than you," he says. "I hope you know that."

"Thank you," I tell him. "I don't think I could have done it without your support."

"Yes, you could have. I know you, Scout—you're a lot more badass than you give yourself credit for."

I feel the heat creep into my cheeks. "Well, thank you. You're pretty badass yourself. I know the season's over, but you guys got so far in the postseason!"

"Yeah, but we didn't get the Cup."

"You can't get every Cup. That doesn't mean you didn't kick ass."

"That goal against Tampa was incredible, huh?" He looks so proud of himself, as he should be. It's the goal that had them winning the tied series and moving on to the next round. They ultimately lost in Game Seven, but it was still a hard-fought series.

"It was pretty hot."

"Hot, huh?"

"Oh, so hot. You know, when Harper said hockey makes her horny, I thought she was nuts, but I get it now."

"Okay, first, I love it when you talk about being horny for me and for hockey. However, I'd rather not know that information about Harper and Wright."

I laugh. "That's fair. That'd be like me getting information about Stevie and—"

"Ah! No. Stop right there. I don't want to hear that info either."

"Can you believe they're together?"

"It was the last thing I ever expected, that's for certain."

"Me too. I thought she was done after Macie's dad, but here she is. Here *they* are."

"Wild year, huh?"

"The wildest," I agree.

"There's my girl!" my dad shouts, shoving Miller out of the way and wrapping his arms around me.

I laugh as I hug him back, and Miller stands over my dad's shoulder, shaking his head with a grin.

"Hey, Dad. Where's Ernesto?"

My dad points over to the dessert table, where his boyfriend is carefully picking over the sugary treats with Macie. For every treat Ernesto puts on his plate, he puts one on hers. They're both piled high, and I don't envy whoever is watching her this evening.

"Peas in a pod, those two," he comments with a grin on his face. He was resistant to Ernesto's advances at first and they took it slow, but now they're inseparable. I know for a fact Ernesto is going to ask my father to move in with him because he asked for my permission first, something I thought was unnecessary but still adorable.

"He loves her," I say, then I peek up at him. "And you."

"Yeah, I know. He's not the only one falling in love with a Thomas." My dad gives Miller a pointed glance then looks over at Stevie, who is currently in the arms of a Comets player, being dipped backward. "Seems like we've had a streak of good luck lately, especially you, Little Miss Published Author. I'm proud of you."

"Thanks, Dad. I'm proud of me too."

"And Pops is too." He puts his hand over his heart. "I can feel it."

Tears spring to my eyes, but I will myself to not cry. "I feel it too."

And I mean that. I've continued going to therapy and stepping out of my comfort zone. I still have times when I want to retreat and times when the grief is just too much, but I push through it and always make it out okay on the other side.

Having my books to escape into helps, as does having Miller around. I hated pushing him away before, but I think it was for the best. I needed to find myself before I gave a piece of me away to someone else.

"Well, I just wanted to check on you. I'm sure you have to make the rounds and want to get back to your friends. Ernesto and I are heading out after he's done with that plate. I'm putting an end to it before he gets sugar sick like at your first book launch." Dad shakes his head, but I know he loves his boyfriend.

"Thanks for coming."

He looks offended. "Like I'd ever miss this." He plants a kiss on my head then shakes Miller's hand. "Always good to see you, son."

Just like every time he says it, Miller lights up when my father calls him *son*. It's sweet and a little sad, but I'm happy that even though Miller has a crappy relationship with his own parents, he doesn't have that with mine.

"Likewise, Dan."

With one last quick hug, my dad takes off, and Miller wraps his arm back around me.

"He's right, you know—Ernesto isn't the only one falling for a Thomas."

"That so?"

"That's so. I still fall for you every day."

"That's a really cheesy thing to say, Miller."

"What can I say? I think your romance novels are rubbing off on me."

Miller, the ever-supportive man that he is, insists on reading my books for authenticity from a sports dude's perspective. I won't lie, his insight has come in handy, not to mention it's kind of fun to have someone to map out the sex scenes with.

"You love them."

"I love *you*," he says, dragging me closer into his arms, wrapping them around my waist and sliding them dangerously low. I know for certain if we weren't in a crowded room right now, he'd already have his hands on my ass. "I can't wait to slide this *forest green* dress off you tonight."

"I can't wait to let you slide it off."

He dips his head, lips at my ear. "I can't wait to see you on your knees staring up at me when we get inside."

My heart pounds, and a shiver races down my spine at his words.

"Inside *our* apartment," he adds, and another shudder runs through me as he dips his hands just an inch lower.

I was already spending all of my time at Miller's place anyway, so we made it official two weeks ago. It's been two weeks full of nonstop sex, and I'm so not complaining.

"Are you allowed to leave your own party early?" he whispers, his lips ghosting over the shell of my ear then down across my neck. "There are so many things I want to do to you tonight, Scout."

Another tremor. "I'm sure there are rules against it, but I kind of don't care right now."

"Kind of?"

"Definitely not. Do not care at all."

"That so?"

More kisses, and my knees begin to shake.

"You have to stop," I groan.

"I don't…"

Kiss.

"…think…"

Kiss.

"…I can."

I shift my hands up his neck, running them through the ends of his hair, tugging until he's looking at me with hazy, lust-filled golden eyes. "Then take me home, Grady."

A deep growl moves through his chest, and my wish gets granted.

I finally get my happily ever after.

. . .

**

Thank you for reading **SCORING CHANCE**!
I hope you enjoyed Miller & Scout.

Want more Carolina Comets?
GLOVE SAVE (Greer's book) is up next!

Need more Miller & Scout?
Keep reading for a bonus scene!

BONUS SCENE

Miller

I can say without a doubt that I have never been happier in my life.

It doesn't matter that I haven't talked to my parents in six months since I finally got the courage to tell them to butt out of my life. It doesn't matter that I broke my wrist and had to miss eight weeks last season. And I don't even care that we didn't make it to the Final.

Nothing can get better than this moment right now.

"Why are you smiling at me like that?"

The grin in question widens even more, especially with Scout's smiling back at me over her shoulder.

She's standing in front of the mirror as she slides a pair of gold hoops through her ears. It's all she's wearing. The earrings, I mean.

She's naked, and I fucking love it.

In the time we've been together, she's grown so much more confident being undressed around me, and it's the biggest damn turn-on ever.

The urge to get out of bed and wrap my arms around her is strong, but I also like watching her. I like how she's not afraid of her belly jiggling or her stretch marks on display. She doesn't care about how her stomach folds every time she bends or how her tits hang lower than she'd like.

She's fucking gorgeous.

And she's all mine.

"Because."

Her brow lifts. "Because why?"

"Because I really want to fuck you right now."

"Miller!"

"What?" I lift a shoulder. "It's true."

"I'm sure it is, but we're running late. In fact, you shouldn't even still be in bed right now. We need to get going, or we'll be late for Macie's game. I'm not sure I want to face that wrath."

She's right that I shouldn't still be in this bed right now, though not for the reason she thinks.

I swing the blanket off me and rise from the bed. Instead of heading for the bathroom to shower and get ready like I know I really need to, I stalk toward what I really want—Scout.

Her eyes widen when she realizes this, and she backs up, but it's pointless. She has nowhere to go.

She's shaking her head at me, but all I can do is grin.

"Miller... We're late."

"So, then we can be later."

"No."

"Yes," I say, gripping her hips and hauling her to me.

She sighs the second her body presses against mine, and being that I'm only in my boxer briefs, there's no hiding the reaction my cock is having to our proximity.

I don't bother wasting a single second capturing her mouth with mine. I kiss her hard and fast and sweet and slow until she's melting into me and I'm melting into her. It's too much and not enough all at the same time.

"Miller..." she groans against me as I bury my face into her neck, kissing and nipping at her as my hands roam over her body, touching every inch. "We're going to be—"

"Late, I know. You said that already. I just don't care. And when I bury my face between your thighs until you're screaming my name and cumming on my tongue, I don't think you'll care much, either."

I feel her knees buckle and catch her effortlessly. I spin her around, backing her toward our bed, gently shoving at her shoulders until she's seated right on the edge.

Then, I drop to my knees, and I devour her.

She sighs when my tongue sweeps over her. Groans when I bury it inside. Cries out when I suck her clit into my mouth.

She doesn't stop rocking against me or making the

sweetest fucking sounds I've ever heard until her thighs are shaking around my head.

"Grady, Grady, Grady," she chants, gripping my hair and holding me to her as she comes apart on my tongue.

She tastes like fucking heaven, and if I died right now, it would be the sweetest death.

When her shivers subside and her grip on my hair loosens, I give her one last kiss before pulling away. I sit back on my haunches with a grin, loving how out of breath she is and the shine coating her skin.

I did that.

"Stop gloating," she says, swatting at me, though there's no malice behind it. She couldn't move right now if she really wanted to.

"I'm not gloating."

"Yes, you are."

"Fine. I am. But it's warranted."

"That so?"

I lift a brow, and she laughs.

"Fine. It's warranted," she concedes. She peers down at my cock that is aching so fucking bad that I'm legit afraid it's about to fall off. "Can I help you with that?"

"Nope," I tell her, rising to my feet.

"No? Are you sure?"

"I'm sure. Besides, we're late, remember?"

"Well, yeah, but I don't want to leave you...*unsatisfied.*"

I laugh. "Oh, Scout. You have no idea how much I love eating your pussy, do you?" Her eyes widen when I place my hands on either side of her, caging her in. "Because I do. I love the way you taste. The way you ride my tongue. I love the sounds you make and how those soft-as-fucking-butter thighs feel around my head. So, trust me, I am more than satisfied right now."

Her mouth is dropped open, and her chest is heaving nearly as hard as it was when I was between her legs, but she's not saying anything. She's just looking up at me with wide, surprised eyes.

Then finally, her lips move, and she whispers something quietly.

"What was that?" I ask.

"I said, how the hell did I get so lucky?"

"I'd argue that *I'm* the lucky one."

She throws her head back with a groan. "Stop it. Stop being so perfect."

"What? I'm just being honest."

"I know, and that's the part that's blowing my mind right now. I'm just still not used to…well, *this*. I've never been loved the way you love me."

"And how's that?"

"Wholly and unabashedly. I feel so damn lucky to have you. I finally feel like the main character."

"You're the main character in my life. Hell, you're my whole damn world."

I press a kiss on her head. "No, go get dressed. We're going to be late."

"That's what I told you!" she says, shoving at me lightly until I finally let her up.

"Yeah, but aren't you glad I didn't listen?" I pull her to her feet, where she rests her forehead against mine with a sigh.

"So glad. I love you, Grady."

"I love you more, Scout."

I lied before.

This is the moment I've never been happier.

OTHER TITLES BY TEAGAN HUNTER

A Slice of Love

Cheesy on the Eyes

TEXTING SERIES

Let's Get Textual

I Wanna Text You Up

Can't Text This

Text Me Baby One More Time

INTERCONNECTED STANDALONES

We Are the Stars

If You Say So

HERE'S TO SERIES

Here's to Tomorrow

Here's to Yesterday

Here's to Forever: A Novella

Here's to Now

Want to be part of a fun reader group, gain access to exclusive content and giveaways, and get to know me more?

Join Teagan's Tidbits on Facebook!

Want to stay on top of my new releases?

Sign up for New Release Alerts!

ACKNOWLEDGMENTS

This book wouldn't be possible without the support of these amazing people:

The Marine who is always there when I'm staying up for days at a time to meet a deadline and puts up with my crap. I love you always and forever.

Laurie (the world's best PA & friend). Thanks for keeping my life together for me.

My incredible editing team: Caitlin, Julia, & Julie… you're the best trio ever!

#soulmate Kristann who is always there to give me girl power mojo!

sMother, Miranda, and Lindsey. Best mom and sisters ever!

All the Bloggers, Bookstagrammers, and BookTokers who have taken a chance on me. Your support really does change lives.

My Tidbits on Facebook. I love you so much.

YOU. Thanks for taking a shot on this book. I really hope you loved it.

With love and unwavering gratitude,

Teagan

TEAGAN HUNTER writes steamy romantic comedies with lots of sarcasm and a side of heart. She loves pizza, hockey, and romance novels, though not in that order. When not writing, you can find her watching entirely too many hours of *Supernatural, One Tree Hill*, or *New Girl*. She's mildly obsessed with Halloween and prefers cooler weather. She married her high school sweetheart, and they currently live in the PNW.

www.teaganhunterwrites.com

CPSIA information can be obtained
at www.ICGtesting.com
Printed in the USA
BVHW030220260123
657201BV00014B/114